MAX'S CAMPERVAN CASE FILES BOOK 1

NINJAS AND Nightmares

TYLER RHODES

Copyright © 2024 Tyler Rhodes

All rights reserved. This book or any portion thereof may not be reproduced or used in any manner whatsoever without the express written permission of the author except for the use of brief quotations in a book review.

This is a work of fiction. Names, characters, businesses, places, events and incidents are either the products of the author's imagination or used in a fictitious manner. Any resemblance to actual persons, living or dead, or actual events is purely coincidental.

Dedicated to all the lucky folk who own gazebos with insect mesh and zip up sides. They rock!

Chapter 1

"I'm not sure about this," I told my two best friends, trying to hide my fear.

"Stop being such a big baby and just do it," teased Min, her blue eyes sparkling with mirth.

"I am not being a baby, but it's a big deal."

"Max, it absolutely isn't."

Anxious yipped his agreement from the bench seat in Vee, my 67 VW Campervan, home on wheels, and the love of my life after Min.

"Fine. Hand it over then."

"Here you go." Min grinned, then flung the black and blue chequered shirt at me.

I caught it and reluctantly ducked out of the campervan and stood on the soggy grass, sighing as I gazed at the sky.

"I can't believe it isn't sunny. And now I have to wear all these clothes? I've been in shorts and a vest for months. I can't even imagine what it's like to wear socks."

Min settled on the floor, her legs over the edge, Anxious in her lap as they watched me with amusement.

Anxious barked, the ears of my best buddy and the smartest Jack Russell Terrier I'd ever met bouncing.

"Hey, I am getting a move on," I told him. "And

we've got ages yet until the funfair really gets going. It's always best when it's dark."

"But we were going to go on a few rides while it's still light," Min reminded me. "If a certain someone ever finishes getting ready. Don't forget your socks." She giggled as she threw the rolled-up feet warmers at me.

I stared at my well-worn black Crocs dolefully, wishing things could be different, but knowing the time had finally come.

The seemingly endless warm summer had slowly morphed into a damper autumn, and even though temperatures remained high in the day and we got sunshine on occasion, the heatwave spell had been well and truly broken. We had returned to good old unpredictable, meaning mostly wet and cloudy, British weather.

"Thanks. I guess I need to admit that it's chilly in the evenings now and wrap up warm."

"Max, it's not exactly freezing. It's still warmer than average for the time of year, and you are just wearing cut-offs and a vest. All you're doing is putting a shirt and socks on."

"I know, but it's the principle."

"And what principle is that?" she asked, putting a hand to her red lips and stifling a laugh.

"The principle of me wandering around in next to nothing and getting an awesome tan."

"You're still really dark. Your eyes are basically green, not blue, from all the sun you've had, your hair is well past your shoulders now, and that beard keeps looking at me strangely."

"I said I'd cut it."

"I like it," she mumbled, but then her head snapped up, causing her luscious blond curls to bounce, and she eased forward then stood, revealing her slim legs clad in tight-fitting, faded jeans, and a figure-hugging green cashmere jumper.

"Thanks. Okay, here goes." With a wink to Min, I slid the shirt on, leaving the buttons undone, then sat in my camping chair under the sun shelter that now had become a rain shelter, and pulled on the socks. It felt strange to have my toes wrapped up like this, and yet strangely comforting. I slid on my new Chelsea boots as not dealing with laces made vanlife a little easier as I was always in and out of the camper, then stood and gave my captive audience a twirl.

"Very handsome!" Min clapped as she smiled.

"And very hot already. But at least I'm still in shorts."

"Make the most of it. In another month, we're in for some nasty weather."

"Then I definitely will. Are we ready to go? Everyone excited about the funfair?"

Anxious leapt from the camper and barked in the affirmative.

"I can't wait. I love the funfair so much." Min stepped to me, her five five versus my six one meaning we'd had plenty of jokes about our names and height over the years, but when she stood on tiptoe and I bent to receive her kiss, I felt the familiar tingle and hoped it would last forever. It was only a quick peck, but our eyes remained locked for a long time, and a smile spread slowly across our faces.

"I know what you're thinking, but don't get your hopes up."

"I don't know what you mean." I couldn't stop grinning, though, and she knew I understood.

"Max, it's a few nights to say goodbye to the summer and celebrate the beginning of autumn. It's the biggest funfair in the south, so how could I say no when you invited me?"

"Even if it means us both sleeping in the campervan?" I teased with a cheeky raised eyebrow.

"Yes, and the Rock n Roll bed isn't perfect, but I slept like a log last night. It's big enough."

"It certainly is. Perfect for a cuddle."

"You keep your hands to yourself," she warned, laughing.

"I promise I will. But you wait until next year when we're a proper couple again."

"Remember, no talk about relationships until the year is up. Then we'll see how we feel. We have more than half a year left yet."

"Min, my feelings will never change, but waiting is the right thing to do. Just so we both know we want to be together again. And when my ex-wife finally sees how awesome I am, I'll be ready."

"I know, and I feel the same, but this is too important to rush into. We agreed. Now, are we going or not?"

"Sure thing."

I grabbed my satchel, locked up, then we linked arms as we headed across the damp grass of the field I'd had almost entirely to myself for three days now. Anxious ran off ahead, familiar with every inch of the campsite, but never tiring of tracking the rabbits that remained elusive.

"This is such a lovely site." Min sighed as she smiled at me and we took in the best that the British countryside had to offer. Tucked away up a winding track hugged by ancient dry stone walls, I'd panicked when the going got almost too narrow for Vee, but when I arrived at a squat stone farmhouse with a woman tending to a beautiful cottage style garden that wrapped around the building, it felt like coming home.

"It's beautiful. Leanne has done a fantastic job with this place. It's a shame it opened at the end of the summer season, but I bet it will be packed next year."

"A woman doing things her own way." Min nodded, a sense of pride in her words. We'd hit it off with the owner, Leanne, and it was like we'd known each other for years. "She's worked so hard getting it up and running after inheriting the business. I wonder why it was closed for so long?"

"Her mum used to run it, but it got too much for her, so she closed down. Leanne moved back to help her out but she died before she could see it open again. It's a sad story, but it hasn't stopped her from working hard."

"Everything is perfect. Even the shower and toilet block is nice."

"The cladding on the building means it blends in perfectly. What I love is the fact the campsite wraps around the trees so everyone gets some privacy, but you can still see what's going on in the middle. It's the ideal site."

"It really is. Are you sure it's not too far to walk into town to the fair?"

"You said you wanted to walk. It's about half an hour. Too much?"

"Not at all. I was just checking. I can't wait. I haven't been to the fair for ages, so this is a real treat."

"It'll be great, but don't forget, I'm not going on all the rides."

"Spoilsport!" Min grinned with anticipation and I knew she didn't mind that for some rides she'd be going solo.

Not much scared me, apart from facing up to the mess I'd made of both our lives a year and a half ago when she divorced me, but being spun around and upside down at high speed was certainly second on the list. My stomach agreed, and if I rode on anything too gnarly I felt awful and turned from tanned to green in an instant.

The light rain of earlier had faded, leaving a smattering of indecisive clouds, but as we exited the gate and strode merrily down the lane, the sun won the battle and burst from behind the diminishing clouds, bathing everything in beautiful sunshine.

Birds sang, bees emerged from their hiding places and buzzed about, and the potholed road shone as light bounced off the wet surface, steaming as the rain evaporated.

"Ah, there's nothing like the smell after it stops raining and the sun comes out," I sighed. "Can you smell it?"

"It's perfect. As if it's sunny just for us. I wish it was always like this."

"Me too." I smiled at the most beautiful, patient, understanding, and caring woman I had ever met, meaning what I said. I could stay like this forever, but knew it wasn't to be quite yet. We'd get there soon enough, and in the meantime I was loving my new vanlife where I cooked in a single pot every night and felt connected to the world around me for the first time since I was a carefree young boy who liked to be outside as much as possible. Now I had all that again and sometimes it didn't feel real. That I could live such a life, and go where I wanted, do what I wished, sleep in my tiny house on wheels or outside with the starry sky as my blanket on a warm summer's night.

We chatted and laughed our way down the hill and emerged at the edge of town like the walk hadn't even happened, so lost were we in our good mood. With dusk approaching, the strobing lights of the funfair made it feel truly magical, so we grinned like kids then held hands and hurried into the thick of things, keen to enjoy everything on offer.

"What shall we go on first?" Min's eyes roamed from one extreme torture ride to the next, hopping from foot to foot.

"You adore the funfair, don't you?" I teased, so happy to see her in such high spirits.

"It's the best. I'm addicted to the thrill, I think."

"I'm not, but I am addicted to seeing you happy."

"Oh, Max, that's so sweet."

Still holding hands, and with Anxious staying close, we took our time walking along the transformed high street where rides were set up, kiosks sold drinks and snacks, heavy on the candy floss, and we spied more and more rides down the side streets as we approached the main event outside the town hall.

We paused on the grass to take everything in. People swarmed everywhere, a sea of smiling, happy faces strobing red and blue, green then fiery orange as the lights flashed and voices competed for people's attention blaring over the various tannoy systems while pop music boomed from distorted speakers, the noise almost deafening.

"Anxious, are you okay, buddy?" I asked, bending to check on him.

He glanced from the funfair to me, eyes wide with wonder, and lifted a paw.

"You want me to carry you? Is it too much? Too loud?"

He stood and shook out, as if saying no, then sat and lifted his paw again.

"I'm not sure what he wants," I told Min.

"I think I might have an idea." Min squatted, then pulled a glow stick from her pocket, bent it to activate the magical liquid inside, and Anxious barked with delight, tail wagging as she waved it in front of him.

"He wanted a glow stick?"

"I showed him one yesterday and he liked it. Shall we all wear one?"

"Sure."

Min fastened a green one around his neck, casting an eerie, ghost-like glow on his white and brown patched fur. I had an orange one on my wrist, while Min took a red one, and, seemingly happy, Anxious proudly led the way into the chaos of the funfair on a perfect evening, even if I was wearing sensible boots and a shirt.

The dodgems beckoned, one of the few rides I genuinely enjoyed, but we forewent the temptation and continued our circuit of the dense groups of rides vying for our custom. Screams and shouts of joy mingled with the sound systems, creating a raw cacophony in the sickly sweet, sugar and hotdog-laden air.

"Look, it's a haunted house," Min shouted in my ear.

"I dare you."

"What are we, twelve?" I laughed.

"I double dare you," she taunted.

"What about Anxious? He might get scared."

Min bent and asked, "Anxious, would you like to go into the haunted house? People in costumes will jump out and try to scare us, but it's just for fun."

Anxious yipped in excitement, and to be fair to the little guy he had been in a much smaller one years ago and took it all in his stride.

"Then it's settled," beamed Min. "Hey, is that Moose? It is, isn't it? Look, over there right by the entrance."

I followed Min's finger and sure enough, it was Moose.

"So he is real? After Lydstock and everyone insisting they'd never seen or heard of him, I was worried. How did he do that?"

"Because, like he said, he's a real life, modern day ninja. Let's go and say hello."

Anxious beat us to it and tore off towards the haunted house and the large man standing off to one side in the shadows, his eyes never still. Scanning the crowds, ready to intervene if there was trouble.

We hurried over and arrived just as Moose squatted easily, belying his imposing frame and clearly overweight body, then scooped up the adoring dog and cradled him in his arms as he stroked his belly. Anxious' tongue lolled happily.

"Moose, it's really you," gushed Min, and, unusually for her, hugged him tight.

"Min! And Max! Great to see you guys."

"You too, Moose. It's been a while. Still working security, I see." I hugged the young security guard then stepped back so he could lower Anxious, who sat and wagged happily when Moose rubbed his head then stood.

"Still working for the same security firm, yes. We've

been all over this summer. Did plenty of festivals and a few other bits and pieces. What about you two? Are you back together yet?"

"Not officially, but I'm working on it," I said with a wink.

"Great! Are you going in there?" he asked with a shudder as he turned to glance at the haunted house.

"You bet. You aren't scared, are you?" asked Min.

"Too right I am. Apparently, it's terrifying. It'll give you nightmares."

"Ninjas and nightmares? That's an odd combination."

"I might know a few moves and a few old school secrets, but there's no need to go looking for a fright. I see enough scary things working as a security guard."

"It's just a few blokes dressed up in costumes, isn't it?" I asked. "Maybe a couple of skulls and some spooky music. Things jumping out from walls. The usual."

Moose moved in close and we huddled together as he whispered, "They've got a clown. A killer clown. With an axe." He shuddered again.

"Sounds awesome," laughed Min, clearly keen to get inside.

"Clowns," I shivered, and not from the cold. "Everyone hates clowns."

"Especially after the music festival. That was wild, right?"

"It sure was, and thanks so much for your help then. You disappeared, and nobody could remember you. It was weird."

"I'm a man of mystery," he confided. "I pull a few Jedi mind tricks and nobody can recall ever meeting me or even my name. It's how Moose rolls."

"Let's catch up properly later. You around for the whole evening?" I asked.

"Sure am. This is my spot for another hour, then I

change places, so I'll see you when you come out. If you come out," he warned ominously.

"You're such a joker," said Min, then kissed the big guy on the cheek and dragged me away.

We paid our entrance fee, then took a moment to study the exterior. It was the usual thing with a big sign declaring terror and nightmares would result from entering, the garish front of what in reality was a large trailer connected to another behind it painted with ghouls and ghosts and a rather too lifelike clown with green hair and, yes, an axe. Regardless, Min was beyond keen, so we entered. The door creaked, then slammed shut behind us.

Thinking it best to carry Anxious, I explained it to him and he was more than happy to oblige.

Immediately, we were plunged into darkness as howls came from the cheap speakers. Min laughed, but gripped my arm tight. Lights burst into life, green and sickly, as a skeleton on a pulley system sprang out then slid past, making us both jump. Anxious yawned and looked bored.

We took several steps along the strange sloped floor, the perspective wrong as it rose sharply to a door that turned out to be only large enough to crawl through. I went first, Anxious still in my arms, and something furry and wet slapped into my face, causing me to scream.

"You big baby," Min giggled from behind, then shoved at me to get a move on. A moment later, she yelped as the same thing attacked her, and I laughed. "Serves you right for making fun of me."

I exited into a round room and helped Min out, then I caught the reflection of a terrifying clown in one of the full-length mirrors. He had a wicked grin and was wielding an axe, ready so strike, his red nose and impossibly large smile glowing with the dull red light that bathed us. Smoke came from machines, pooling around our ankles, but it was a half-hearted affair and petered out as I spun to confront the clown, but he'd vanished.

"Where'd he go? " I asked.

"No idea. Come on, let's go that way." Min led us through a wonky doorway and we found ourselves in another passage.

A scream rang out, sending shivers down my spine. Min squeezed my arm tighter and said, "Wow, that sounded real. Like someone is genuinely being attacked."

"It did. Think we should investigate? It came from over there." I pointed to the end of the passage, so we smiled, then ran to discover what lame fright awaited us.

I pulled up short when Min suddenly stopped, her eyes wide, hand to her mouth in shock.

"That's so realistic." I noted the crumpled body on the bare boards, turned on its side with a pool of blood spreading out towards us down the slope.

"It really is. Good job," Min congratulated the actor.

They didn't move, and I knew this wasn't right, so stepped forward, mindful of the fake blood, and squatted beside the body of what I now believed was a woman.

Anxious growled, and as I put my hand on her shoulder to check on her, she rolled onto her back. Anxious launched from my arms and landed in the blood, skidded, then scrambled back, slapping sticky footprints in his wake.

"That's great effects," said Min, a tinge of nerves in her voice.

"Min, it's Leanne. The campsite owner."

"Oh, hello. Didn't know you worked here."

"She doesn't."

"But if she doesn't work here, why's she got a fake axe sticking out of her chest?" Min frowned, and then it dawned on her. "Oh no! It can't be real."

We had to face the truth. It was real blood, and a real axe, and it was embedded in Leanne's chest.

I checked for a pulse, even lifted an eyelid, but we were too late.

Leanne was dead. Murdered in a haunted house.

The clown raced past, giggling like a madman, and he wasn't holding his axe.

I grabbed Min and wrapped her in my arms, then bent over to protect her as best I could.

What a way to go out. And I hadn't even tried the candy floss.

Chapter 2

"Why are you bent over like that? " asked a very squeaky voice.

I turned and stared into the heavily made-up eyes of the clown. He smiled, which made him even more terrifying, the painted lips in a perpetual grin that screamed, "I will murder you!"

Gradually, things clicked into place, and I asked warily, "You aren't going to try to murder us?"

"What you on about, mate? It's just a bit of fun, isn't it? You alright? That your missus? She's shaking. You okay, love? Is this bloke molesting you? Are you one of them pervy dudes that hang around in haunted houses to grab a feel? That ain't right, and I won't stand for it."

The clown puffed out his chest, the garish yellow shirt with a collar up to his ears hardly terrifying, at least on anyone apart from a clown. He ruffled his ill-fitting green wig of tight curls and it slid sideways over an eye, so he straightened it with a cheesy grin.

"No, I'm fine. He's my husband. Um, ex-husband. Er, look, can't you see what's happening here?"

"Ah, there it is," exclaimed the clown with relief. "Thought I'd lost it." He bent to the axe, then gasped as Min and I moved aside and Anxious barked a warning, causing the clown to scream, fall back onto his bum, his blue dungarees rising up high to reveal more of his oversized comedy shoes.

"Best not touch the axe," I cautioned.

"Was it you?" asked Min, scooting away from what I now realised was a young man in his twenties with acne showing through the make-up.

"Is she... Is that... Did you... Hey, what's the deal?" he hissed, eyes darting from me to Min then back again.

"That's your axe, isn't it?" I asked.

"Course it isn't! I dropped it somewhere a minute ago. Then the lights went out and I couldn't find it. But mine's not real. It's fake. Can't be wielding a real axe in here and killing the punters." His eyes drifted to the body of Leanne and he balked then turned away.

Min and I stood and watched the clown cautiously —there was no telling if he was lying or not. I believed he was being truthful, but it didn't mean I wasn't wary.

"You could be lying," stammered Min. "You might attack us."

"But I haven't got my axe, and it's fake like I said. We need to get out of here. There's a murderer on the loose and we might be next. Unless," the clown's eyes widened, "it was you two. Did you kill her?"

"Of course we didn't," I said.

"You were right by the body. Bent over and looking guilty."

"I was protecting Min from you. I thought you were the killer."

"That was so heroic." Min stared at me with adoration, and my heart swelled with pride.

"You know I'd do anything to keep you safe. And right now, this freaky clown is right. We need to get out of here. But we need to be quick, and ensure the killer doesn't escape. Let's go. Lead the way." I pointed to the clown.

"Me? Why me?"

"Because you know the quickest way out. Is there

more than one?"

"The front door, and there's a fire escape, but that's hidden unless there's an emergency. Let's go the front way. Oh, I'm Chuck."

"I'm Max, and this is Min. That's Anxious."

"I don't blame him. So am I."

I sighed, but forewent an explanation as now wasn't the time, and we rushed after a fast-retreating Chuck as he raced off.

"Anxious, you stick with us. Don't get lost," I warned.

He kept between us as we ducked through a low doorway, down the sloping floor, and out into the wild night. The sights, sounds, and smells were beautiful, as it meant we were alive.

"Moose, did anyone come out before us?" I shouted as we spied him on duty.

"Hey, guys. What's up? Looks like it scared you for real in there. That good, eh?"

"Moose, there's a dead woman inside. She got axed. Like, literally. We thought it was this guy, but he swears it wasn't him. But he had an axe earlier, and now one's in poor Leanne."

"Leanne?"

"She runs, I mean ran, the campsite we're staying at. She's dead."

"Then you better stay right where you are, sir." Moose's arm shot out too fast to see and gripped Chuck, his large hand completely covering the slim man's shoulder.

"Hey, get off me!" Chuck tried to shrug Moose off, but the much bigger man held him fast.

"I won't hurt you, but we need to ensure you don't escape until we sort this out. Max, what should I do with him?"

"Do you promise to wait until the police arrive?" I asked Chuck.

"Why should I? I didn't do anything wrong."

"You were first on the scene, sir, and are a suspect. You were inside when the woman died. You can't leave."

"Chuck, he's right. Will you stay if Moose releases you?"

"What's with you all? How do you know each other? Maybe you did it," Chuck accused Moose, looking utterly freaked out.

"I was outside, on duty. Max, Min, are you both okay? You didn't get hurt?"

"We're fine, thanks, and I'm sure Chuck is innocent. Maybe let him go?" I suggested.

With a shrug, Moose released his captive and shuddered as he studied the shaking clown. Even ninja men of mystery couldn't handle clowns, it seemed. Moose rubbed his hands on his black cargo trousers, the shiny boots, black polo shirt, and high-viz vest giving him a menacing air. He exuded a military vibe at odds with his kind nature and almost high-pitched Birmingham accent. His youthful face belied how skilled he was, but I recalled the way he moved and how he had demonstrated his fighting skills and was in no doubt about how competent he truly was.

Chuck moved to bolt, but Moose jumped into his path, and Chuck gasped.

"How did you do that? You were over there a moment ago. That's freaky, man."

"Don't run," I warned. "Moose will catch you."

"A fat guy like him?" laughed Chuck. "I'm slim and speedy. No chance."

Moose stepped away from Chuck, coughed to get his attention, then we all gasped as Moose appeared behind Chuck.

Moose tapped him on the shoulder and the bewildered man spun and screamed in fright and shock, "No way! That's unreal. You gotta teach me, dude. Please?"

"Some of the old ways are secret," said Moose softly, a faraway look in his eyes, as if recalling his training.

"Moose, can you keep an eye on things here while Chuck shows us the back door? We need to act fast in case anyone escapes from inside. Maybe the killer is still in there."

"Sure, no problem. I didn't see anyone leave before you, so maybe you're right."

"I'll wait here," said Min. "You take Anxious. And Max?"

"Yes?"

"Be careful."

"You too." With a nod, we followed Chuck, who was more than keen to get away from Moose and his strange ways.

As we chased around the side of the haunted house, I called the police and explained what had happened then hung up before I got asked questions I didn't have the time to answer.

The massive haunted house seemingly folded out from a flatbed. How it collapsed in on itself I couldn't fathom, and now wasn't the time for an engineering lecture, so I kept an eye on Chuck as he clambered up a small set of metal steps and waited for us.

Anxious put one paw on the steps than whined and backed up—his tiny feet could get stuck and he knew it.

"You keep guard here," I suggested. I joined Chuck and asked, "Can you lock it?"

"No way, dude, that's against the rules. What if there's a fire? People need to get out. And anyway, if the murderer is inside, what if he attacks the others?"

"There are more people in there? Why didn't you say? We can't leave them alone with whoever did this. You wait here. If anyone comes out, take their photo but don't try to stop them. You might get hurt."

With a call for Anxious, I raced back to the front,

explained to the others that there might be people inside, then approached the booth and asked the bored-looking woman sipping on a coffee if she knew how many people were in the haunted house then explained about the murder.

"Murder! What are you talking about? I just saw you with Chuck and assumed he was taking a break. It's been quiet so far and only you and your lady friend went in recently."

"What about the woman who was killed? She runs the campsite I'm staying at and she was in there."

The ticket seller leaned forward, causing me to take a step back as the smell of her perfume was so strong, and with narrowed eyes she snapped, "Then she shouldn't have been. I ain't sold a ticket to anyone else in half an hour as the haunted house don't get busy until later. And I didn't sell one to no woman. Just a couple of lads earlier, and that's it."

"But could someone still be inside?"

"I guess. The dead woman was." She shrugged as if it was nothing but an inconvenience.

"Do you control things from here? The lights and everything?"

"I press a few buttons, sure. It's all wired up to here."

"Then can you shut everything down? Turn the lights on inside, stop the spooky stuff? And I'm Max. What's your name?"

"They call me Sheena. You ain't the cops, are you? Why should I do what you say?"

"I'm not telling you, I'm asking," I said, trying to retain my cool but feeling the stress of the situation begin to take over. "If there's someone inside, they might be in danger. I'm going in to check, and want to be able to see. Is that okay?"

"Sure, but I'm calling Lash, the boss. He'll know what to do. But I'll turn up the lights for now. There's really been a murder?"

"There has, and we don't want another one." I hurried back to Min and Moose, then said I was going back inside.

"Max, you can't. It's too dangerous."

"And what if someone's in there and the killer's after them? I have to. Moose, will you look after Min?"

"I'll come with you. Min, you'll be safe here. Just don't stop anyone that comes out."

"No, I'm coming too." Min stomped her foot and crossed her arms. I knew better than to argue.

Anxious barked, insisting on coming, too, so together we approached the now thankfully quiet haunted house, the lights still flashing but no music blared. I opened the door, and now the automated systems were off there was no squeal and it didn't slam shut behind us.

"We should stick together," said Moose, his size meaning he took up almost the width of the peculiar sloping corridor.

"Good idea. It isn't very big anyway," I said, strangely comforted by the big guy's presence.

Anxious led the way, retracing our steps, and soon we came to Leanne. The blood had already begun to dry in the stifling heat, and a skin had formed over it, making it look like jelly. Moose said nothing, and we continued along the corridor, turned, and seemingly looped back on ourselves then onto the corridor Chuck had led us out through, but we checked each side passage, several rooms which would have undoubtedly held a few surprises if the automated frights were on, but looked sad and cheap in the harsh white light.

We spotted Chuck's axe on the floor of the passage and it was obviously fake, but we left it alone in case it was evidence, and discovered nothing else of interest. We called out repeatedly to be sure, and after nobody answered we returned to the back door and opened it, causing Chuck to leap back and raise his hands as he shouted, "Don't murder me!"

"It's me, Max. Can you come in? We didn't find anyone, but I want to be sure we check every corridor and room."

"Um, I guess." He shrugged, but entered cautiously and toured us around the interior, but we'd seemingly seen all there was to see and five minutes later we exited through the front door, having found nothing. Chuck had picked up his axe and was holding it tight to his chest like it might ward off an attack.

Sheena left her booth, locked it, then joined us. I made the introductions, then Min asked a very important question. "Does anyone else work inside, or is it just Chuck?"

Sheena and Chuck exchanged a worried look, then she said, "Sure, there's Gaz, but he doesn't start for an hour yet. Like I said, it's beyond quiet until late, and we haven't been open long. Gaz is a zombie. Gives the punters a real scare," she laughed.

"He's terrifying," agreed Chuck. "He works the rides until nine, then joins me. We have a right laugh freaking everyone out. The later it gets, the more fun we have."

"Sorry, but I can't concentrate with you dressed like that," admitted Min. "You're a killer clown with awful makeup, blood-splattered comedy clothes, and it's so sinister."

"It's why I scare everyone so well," said Chuck. "But if it helps, I can take off the wig?" Without waiting for an answer, he removed the garish green wig, revealing a crop of short black hair plastered to his skull with sweat. He rubbed at his forehead and sighed. "Ah, that's better. It's been a killer summer with the heat, but even today I'm burning up. It's intense in there."

"I bet it was awful a week ago when the temperature broke new records," noted Min.

"It sure was. We were further south and it was crazy hot. Had to nip out every ten minutes to cool down. What are we meant to do now?"

"Hopefully nothing. Here's the police now."

We watched a man approach with a middle-aged policeman. Neither looked happy. Whereas the policeman was smart, but carrying a fair amount of extra weight around his middle, with thin arms and legs, Lash was the opposite. A tight stomach with thick limbs, no neck to speak of, and a square head shaved to the bone. He had a wicked scowl on his face.

"What's this about a body, Sheena? You better not be fooling around again. I warned you about that."

"I'm not messing, Lash. This lot found a corpse. Reckon it's some woman."

"What woman?" he asked, staring at us.

"The owner of the campsite I'm staying at. A woman named Leanne," I explained.

"And you're sure she's dead?" asked Lash with an unfriendly glare at me.

"Sir, I'll ask the questions from now on," said the officer. He introduced himself, asked everyone to wait while I showed him where the body was, and without preamble I did exactly that.

He called it in immediately, although I assumed the police were already on their way in force, then spoke to his boss before we joined the others. We were asked to wait by the booth while he checked more thoroughly once another officer arrived to ensure nobody came out unexpectedly.

He came out shaking his head, so he and the other officer set up a cordon around the haunted house then did the same at the rear, reeling the tape out around the entire structure.

Lash grumbled the whole time, lamenting the loss of business as more and more people came to see what was happening, morbid curiosity always strong once the crime scene tape went up. I knew from way too much experience that it drew people in their droves, the desire to discover what happened stronger than the attractions blaring promises of thrills and guarantees of no spills.

Min, Moose, Anxious, and I moved away from the funfair folk who were bickering about what they should do, and once out of earshot, Min asked, "Could it be one of them?"

"Possibly," I conceded, "but Chuck's taking a massive risk if it was him. He was the only other person inside besides us, so will be the prime suspect. And he seems too timid to be murdering with an axe. He's barely out of his teens."

"Teens kill all the time, unfortunately," lamented Moose. "Knives mostly. It's an epidemic in some parts of the country."

"I know, and that's terrible, but Chuck doesn't seem the type. He was rattled by this, but yes, it might be an act." I took a moment to study the group of three. Chuck was a lanky young man, still filling out his frame, a fresh-faced youth with his entire future ahead of him. It was impossible to know exactly what he looked like because of the clown make-up, besides messy black hair; the rest was anyone's guess.

Sheena was a scrawny woman who looked like she'd had a tough life. In her forties, was my estimate, but she'd lived those years hard. Maybe being on the road for decades, with all that entailed for those in the funfair business. She had a tanned, lined face, a few missing teeth, hollow cheeks, with heavy-lidded brown eyes, and thin, straw-coloured hair that hung straight over her shoulders.

Lash, and so far that was the only name I'd got, was easy to get a rise out of, too, judging by the shouting and the shaking fists, and how red his face kept going as he barked at the others. His pale blue eyes were intelligent, though, and there was more going on than you'd first expect with this man, I was sure of it.

"What happens now?" asked Min.

"Now we wait for the police to interview us. A detective will probably arrive soon, but it might just be an officer that questions us. The ambulance should arrive any minute, and I assume there will be several teams to go over the scene. It'll take hours, most likely."

"And we didn't even get to go on the dodgems." Min smiled weakly at her own joke, and I knew she was just trying to lighten the mood.

"Maybe tomorrow?"

"Think they'll keep the fair open tonight?" asked Moose. "I better talk to my boss. Explain what's happened. It's been great to see you guys again, and I'll be back soon, but I better go."

Moose vanished in his usual astonishing way, and Min and I remained where we were, watching as the crowds increased and the police arrived in their droves.

Chapter 3

The place was soon swarming with police, paramedics, and various more specialised teams, all converging on the haunted house. Harsh overhead lights bathed the entire scene as the multi-coloured ones blinked off one by one. The music and shouts of encouragement to buy tickets faded away as rides finished and I assumed were ordered to be shut down.

As the funfair died a slow, painful death, the noise of the customers rose in pitch, everyone complaining about it closing so early, and not knowing why. The haunted house became the prime focus as more and more people heard about the killing, gossip spreading faster than any wild fire ever could, and soon it was bedlam as the crowds grew more animated and began to call for the funfair to be re-instated.

An announcement came over the tannoy system, declaring the site was shut for the rest of the evening so the police could investigate a suspected murder, and people were asked to remain where they were as everyone's details would be taken. The moment the announcement was over, visitors began to leave. Some grumbling about not hanging around for hours as they'd done nothing wrong, others clearly worried and possibly with something to hide, and groups hurried off, with nobody to stop them.

Moose returned to where we were waiting and said, "That was dumb to tell everyone their details would be taken. They should have set up cordons and taken people's information as they left. Now half the visitors have gone already. Dumb."

"I guess they didn't think of that. And they can't really believe they could take everyone's details, could they?" asked Min, watching like us as the crowds thinned and more people hurried off in all directions.

"It's unlikely," I said. "I don't think it's usual to do that either. There are too many people here, and as Moose said, there's no way to stop everyone just leaving now."

The police tried to roll out tape to block people, but it soon became apparent to the officers that it was a lost cause, and they resorted to standing at the various exits and stopping as many visitors as they could.

"They're utterly unorganised," I noted with a frown. "Why hasn't someone told them what to do?"

"Beats me," said Moose. "We haven't even been asked to help out. I'm assuming that nobody's taken charge yet."

"They need to. It's utter chaos. Look at them."

Officers tried, and failed, to get the details of people walking across the grass towards the high street, or leaving by any number of other side streets, but it was obviously impossible in such a large space.

Several had been tasked with getting the details of those who remained, so went up to people individually before asking them to leave the area. But it wasn't working well, as many refused to give their information, so arguments erupted before the officers accepted that they could never handle this. They soon gave up, and within minutes almost the entire funfair was deserted bar a group of determined onlookers crowded around the haunted house, over a dozen police officers, the teams working the scene, paramedics waiting to remove the body, and the funfair workers.

"Wow, look how many people work here," noted Min as a group converged at the dodgems. "There must be at least thirty of them, if not more."

"It's one of the biggest funfairs in the country, so probably has more than that," said Moose. "I know most of them. They're good people, some of the best, but it's a gruelling life."

"Have you been doing security with them for long?"

"For years on and off. We usually do a stint in the summer when they're busiest, but they travel for nine months of the year then have three months off. A lot of them live together at a travellers' site. They have caravans that they live in all year round. They get towed everywhere."

"Is there usually much trouble?" I asked.

"More than there should be." Moose shook his head sadly, and sniffed. "It's a shame, but a lot of the workers are from the travelling community, and there are still plenty of people who think they're trouble. They aren't, no more than anyone else, but they see more than their fair share of grief, sure."

"Like what? Name-calling? Fights? Worse?"

"Nothing worse, at least not for a few years. Usually, it's fights with drunk groups who pick on one of the men. It begins with a few crossed words and escalates. The men here, and the women, have hard lives and won't let an insult stand. It's their way, and how it's always been."

"What about feuds between themselves? Any bad blood?"

"Isn't there always when people spend so much time together and have high-stress situations all the time? But nothing too serious. Just the usual fallings out and disagreements. But hey, I work security, and don't know everything that goes on." Moose shrugged.

"Come on, Moose, it's us. We know you, and I'm positive you know everything that goes on. With your ninja skills, I bet you hear all the gossip," I teased.

"Maybe I do," he laughed, smiling. "But they're decent, hard-working people just trying to get by the same as the rest of us. I don't judge."

"Of course not, and neither do we," said Min. "Hey, what's happening now?"

We turned to watch two women approach Lash and his staff at the booth. Lash snapped something and they tried to pacify him, but he shrugged them off and shouted, then pointed at us. All attention turned our way before the women spoke briefly with all three then approached.

Anxious, who had become bored and was lying on my foot to make a point about the funfair being rubbish, snapped to attention as they got close. I could smell fast food, possibly burgers, the aroma of fried onions strong, and Anxious clearly picked up more than me as he snorted then stood, tail wagging, attention fixed on both women's hands.

Each held a carton and kept glancing at them as they chatted quietly before stopping in front of the sniffing guard dog.

"I think he can smell your dinner," I chuckled. "You'll have a friend for life if he gets a taste. So be warned. He'll follow you everywhere."

"Aw, what a sweetie," said the younger of the two women. She wore a bizarre one-piece grey jumpsuit like you'd see in an early eighties movie, with curled hair stiff with so much product it didn't move at all. Heavy, green eyeshadow and plenty of lipstick completed the look, but she was smiling and had laughter lines, so clearly was a positive type.

"So adorable," agreed her partner, a woman who must have been in her late sixties and dressed in an outfit straight from Marks and Spencer. Smart black slacks, a simple white blouse, and a lightweight cardigan, with sensible shoes. Her slim figure and toned look indicated she exercised hard, too, but like her partner she had a friendly demeanour and a kind face. I liked them instantly.

Both bent and fussed over the prancing dog, who rested his paws on their legs and panted happily. I knew his game, and it paid off almost immediately as the pair opened their containers then looked up and asked me, "Is it okay?"

"Sure," I laughed, thinking they were like twins the way they spoke at the same time. When they made the exact same movement, and offered Anxious a piece of burger simultaneously, they both chuckled then let him enjoy his impromptu snack before closing the containers and standing, their attention now on us.

"So, here we are," beamed the younger woman.

"We are indeed," agreed the older lady.

"Are you both detectives?" asked Min when they weren't more forthcoming, merely smiled at us as though waiting for an invitation to speak.

"Yes!" they both agreed, then burst out laughing.

"You first," said jumpsuit lady.

"Thank you. Now, we understand that you three, along with the freaky clown, were the first on the scene and that you," she pointed at me and Min, "and that terrifying young man we just spoke to, were the first to see the body? Is that correct?"

"Yes, that's correct," I said.

"Great!" they both barked, finding it hilarious.

The elder said, "I'm Susan, and this is Susan too. To save any confusion, call me Susie, and my partner Sue. Are you all following so far?" We agreed we were. "We are both detective sergeants, and have been partners for many years, so have been around. Don't let our looks fool you. We know the deal, and won't stand for any nonsense."

"Absolutely none," agreed Sue. "She may look like a granny, and I know I look like I stepped out of Flashdance and you may think I'm strange, but I've got news for you. I don't care!"

Both women beamed at us, nodded to each other, then Sue ushered Min and Moose to one side while Susie remained with me. I didn't know what to think about this strange pair, who seemed extremely close to each other and clearly had worked together for many years judging by how they were so in-tune with one another. What I didn't yet know was what they thought about me, and how they'd take it once they found out how many murder mysteries I'd already been involved in.

Sometimes I found it hard to believe myself. But trouble found me no matter where I went, and now I had accepted that this was my role in life. A vanlifer turned amateur detective with a real knack for solving mysterious murders. I'd managed to figure out each case now, and knew we'd be embroiled in this one if for no other reason than because Min and I had enjoyed Leanne's company. We admired her spirit and determination to make the campsite such a wonderful place to stay.

"Hello? Earth to mystery man." Susie smiled as she waved her hand in front of my face.

"Sorry. I was just wondering what you'll think of me once you know who I am."

"Now that's piqued my interest. And exactly who are you, sir?"

"Max Effort. A lot of detectives seem to know all about me when I introduce myself. It's often an issue, but I promise that—"

"Sue, it's him! It's really him. So that means you're talking to the famous Min! And look, it's Anxious. The dog that helps solve the mysteries."

Sue spun and grabbed Min in a tight hug then dragged her over to us with Moose bringing up the rear, smiling at the excitement.

"Wow! I wasn't expecting that," I told Susie.

"We love your work, Max. Min's too. We follow all your cases. The last one was a real doozy."

"Incredible," agreed a rather flushed Sue as she stared at us like we were royalty. "The way you solved those apparent suicides was nothing short of spectacular, and we heard all about how disgruntled the lead detective was. You put his nose right out of joint."

"He should have been more thorough," said Susie.

"He should have," agreed Sue. "Min, you were at Chucklefest, weren't you?"

"Um, yes. It was very intense, but Max figured it out."

"So did you, and a young woman we befriended. The detective, a man named Dee, was also very helpful. He let us ask questions and look into the murders."

"It sounded awesome!" gushed Susie. "And now you're here."

"It's our lucky day," laughed Sue. "Max, what's your secret, eh? Everyone wants to know. How do you do it? How do you solve seemingly impossible to solve crimes?"

"It's because he's an ex-chef," said Moose. "Max used to work in Michelin 3-star restaurants and was one of the best chefs in the country. He has an incredible eye for detail and picks up on the slightest thing. I worked with both these guys at Lydstock and we caught the killer."

"You're the infamous Moose?" the two Susans asked, eyes wide. "We thought you were nothing but an urban myth? We read Max's wiki page and you were mentioned, but apparently nobody else even remembers your name or what you look like."

"That's me. Moose. And as to why nobody remembers me, well, I can't give away all my secrets."

"He's a ninja," noted Min.

"He really is," I agreed, caught up in this strange high-energy conversation.

"So it's true?" asked the Susans.

Sue stepped closer to Moose and asked, "But how did you make everyone forget you? That makes no sense. You're a security guard. Surely your boss and fellow workers know you and can recall your name?"

"Maybe they can, maybe they can't. Maybe once this

is over, you won't recall this conversation at all," he said cryptically, shrugging.

"We like you," squealed the Susans.

"Now, Max, is this really how you do it? You have a keen eye for detail? That's how you solve your cases?" asked Susie.

"Usually. Someone will let something slip, or I recall someone doing something, or notice something that's off and my subconscious seems to put the pieces together gradually."

"And now you're working with us! How incredible. What a treat," gushed Sue.

"I am?"

"Sure you are," said Susie. "A lovely lady's been murdered in cold blood and you and Min were right there when it happened. It's our lucky day." Susie actually rubbed her hands together, and her smile was worryingly wide. It was hard to see how they were long-standing DSs as they were so unusual in their behaviour and certainly their attitude towards us.

"Just so there's absolutely no confusion, are you saying that you want our help?"

"Of course!" they agreed, laughing and nodding.

"Me too?" asked Moose.

"Yes, the three of you."

Anxious barked, and wagged his tail, causing them both to giggle.

"And Anxious the wonder dog," they agreed.

Anxious yipped that he was in.

"Now, I suppose we better take statements. Let's get that out of the way first, then we can talk about what happens next.

After we broke into groups again and gave our statements, describing what we saw and what happened after we found Leanne, we joined up again and the detectives simply stared at us, everyone else seemingly forgotten for now.

Sue explained what came next. "We'll question everyone involved, which isn't many people now as we already spoke to the owner, the clown, and Sheena at the ticket booth, but we'll see what we uncover. But first we'll go over the scene slowly and properly, just in case anything's been missed, then the body can be released."

"And we want you to keep your eyes and ears open for anything strange," said Susie, taking up where Sue left off. "Obviously, someone knows something, but this scene wasn't handled very well before we arrived and most visitors have left. They shouldn't have shut the fair down until we were ready to block off the exits and could take everyone's details. But it's done now, and mostly doesn't matter."

"Because the killer is probably someone who would appear innocent anyway," I suggested.

"Yes, exactly! Ah, it's begun. Max is beginning to think about the case and who did it and why. That's what we'll be doing. We'll look into Leanne's past, see if she had any enemies, check the axe for fingerprints, all the usual stuff, but what we really need are people on the ground who can ask around and won't rile anyone." Sue grinned at us, her good humour contagious despite the seriousness of the situation.

"So, can we go now?" asked Min.

"Of course. But don't you want to examine the body in more detail?" asked Sue.

"You're okay with that?" asked Min, astonished.

"Absolutely. The more the merrier," said Susie, wrapping her cardigan around her, a habit she performed repeatedly.

With a shrug, we followed the ladies as they cleared a path by shouting at anyone in their way, and a more incongruous sight I had never seen. A lady approaching her retirement years and an eighties-addicted woman in her mid-thirties running the entire scene with a firm grip and everyone doing what they were told.

We ducked under the tape and entered the haunted house yet again. The place was swarming with police and specialists, every corridor and room crowded, but they moved aside as our merry band approached the victim and left us after a curt word from the Susans.

Without the stress of wondering if we might be murdered next, the scene was utterly transformed. I noted Leanne's tattoo on her bare forearm, but it looked almost smudged, and when I mentioned this the detectives were beside themselves with glee. They got it photographed then wiped at it, cleaning up Leanne's dirty arm. Her jeans were stylish ripped ones, her boots a hard-wearing work variety, and her dark plait was wrapped around her neck like it had been trying to strangle her.

The axe itself was a basic model I assumed could be bought in any number of DIY stores. Nothing remarkable about it, and certainly nothing like the oversized fake one Chuck had wielded. This was used more for splitting kindling than anything else, but it was still a very deadly weapon.

"Did she have her phone and wallet on her?" I asked.

"No wallet or purse, but many people don't carry one these days," said Sue. "We have her phone and keys, though, and that was it. No jewellery, not even a ring, which is suspicious."

"She told us that she never wears any," said Min. "She was always losing them while she worked on the campsite, so never bothered."

"Then that's one mystery solved," said Susie, clapping her hands and smiling yet again.

We stayed a while longer, but there was nothing that caught my eye and nothing to explain how or why she'd been attacked. There was no sign of a struggle, no clues to bag and examine, and absolutely no sign of the killer.

We exchanged numbers with the detectives, and promised to be in touch the next day, then left them to it.

Outside, we chatted with Moose for a while and swapped details, too, then left him to his work, agreeing to meet up in the morning if he could.

I'd wanted to say goodbye to Chuck, but there was no sign of him.

Chapter 4

"Do you think they'll open the funfair tomorrow?" asked Min, walking alongside me as we left town.

"I think they will, but with the Susan twins I wouldn't be surprised by anything. They are like twins, aren't they?"

"They really are. If they were the same age, then I'd bet money on it. I don't think I've ever met anyone like them before. They want our help, Max. They actually asked us. It's weird to think that you have genuine fans in the police department like that. They talk about you. You're a legend."

"I don't know about that. Actually, it makes me feel uncomfortable to know people are talking about me. I never wanted to be famous, or on TV, or any of that. I'm a private person, you know that, and maybe not shy, but certainly not craving the limelight."

"I know, and I'm sorry you're uneasy about your new fame. But I don't think you have to worry. It's about as niche as you can get. As long as they don't make a TV series about your adventures, you'll never be recognised in the street. Hey, even if they did make a show, you wouldn't be recognised as they'll have an actor playing you. Ooh, I wonder who it'll be?"

"Hugh Grant or Jason Statham?" I suggested with a wink.

Min linked her arm through mine and smiled. "Don't be silly. You need someone younger. An up-and-coming star, most likely. Hmm, I wonder who will play me? And as for this adorable guy," Min nodded to Anxious trotting merrily ahead, "I think he'll be the real star. He could play himself. How cool would that be?"

"Very," I admitted. "But right now our main concern is poor Leanne and the fact someone, for some utterly mad reason, decided to put an axe in her chest in the haunted house. It's about as dumb as you can get. Almost anywhere else would have been easier to get access to, and the risk of being caught was high. So why go to so much trouble?"

Min chewed on her lip in thought, the cute act making me smile although I tried to hide it, then brightened. "It's got to be because she had arranged to meet them there, right?"

"I'm assuming so. It would have still been very risky, but it makes sense. We need to find out who she was meeting."

"And we need to find out why anyone would want to kill her. What worries me is that we were in there with the killer, or missed them by literally a few minutes at most. Nobody saw anyone else leave the haunted house though. Not even Moose. And how awesome is it that he's here? I missed him."

"Me too. He's a great guy, and it's nice to know we aren't going crazy and just imagining him."

"Maybe we are. Maybe he's just in our heads," teased Min, pulling me closer then stopping before standing on tiptoe and kissing my cheek, bashfully brushing a luscious blonde lock from her smouldering eyes.

"Why the kiss? Not that I mind, of course, and the more the merrier, but why did you do that?"

"Because being with you from the start of your latest murder mystery has made me realise how wonderful a man you are."

"You don't know that already?"

"Of course I do. But seeing how you handle things is impressive."

"But I didn't do anything. I was going to say the same to you. I'm very proud of how you coped with such a horrible discovery. Poor Leanne. She was such a lovely woman too."

We continued in silence as we left town and began the walk up the hill back to the campsite. Gone were streetlights and the glare of the funfair. No cars passed, and as it was true night now, the way was lit by nothing but the stars and a crisp waning sliver of moon. Thankfully, the sky was clear, just a wisp of cloud passing over the moon before it vanished. Enough light for us to see the potholed track of compacted gravel but little else.

After ten minutes, Min began to shiver, and kept drawing me closer to her.

"Are you cold? Do you want my shirt?"

"No, I'm not cold, and thanks for the offer. It's this place. I can't see a thing."

"Nothing will happen. Don't be scared." I glanced left then right, then couldn't resist checking behind, but Min was right. The light level was so low that we could only see a few paces in any direction. The high dry stone walls with hedges growing on top in some places made the track very enclosed and blocked the wind, leaving it eerily quiet and as though we were walking through a tunnel.

Min squeezed my arm when a noise startled us, then something furry and fast raced across the track just ahead before vanishing into a gap in the wall.

Min squealed, I jumped, and Anxious barked as he ran to the wall and scratched at the stone, daring the intruder to show itself. We waited while he did what he did best—chase and fail to catch anything—but at least it cheered him up, if not us.

Once he'd grown bored and ran off ahead to continue his mini adventure, we increased our speed, trying to get clear of the oppressive walls where the air felt stagnant and soon became out of breath as the gradient increased.

Suddenly, I paused, causing Min to yelp in confusion, and I put a finger to my lips then spun and peered back the way we'd come, sure I heard footsteps. Was it my imagination, or was there someone on the track with us? Were we being stalked? My imagination began to get the better of me, and I pictured a demonic clown with an axe standing atop the wall, ready to chop our heads off as we passed, or for him to come pelting up the track, arms waving wildly, a deranged look on his smeared clown makeup face. I had to shake my head to clear the vision.

I chuckled, then smiled at Min reassuringly.

"Why are you grinning like a maniac? What did you see?"

"I thought I heard something, but it's just the wind."

"There is no wind here."

"Maybe it was another rabbit or a rat."

"They have rats!?"

"Everywhere has rats, Min. And I'm not looking like a maniac, am I? I was just smiling at you to reassure you."

"Then don't! It's disconcerting." Nevertheless, Min returned the smile to confirm she was joking, then huddled in close as we continued. I kept quiet about the clown!

The steeper the rise, the lower the walls became, until they morphed into hedgerow, then stock-proof fencing as we approached the campsite. We slowed, partly due to the exertion, partly because a sense of unease had begun to fester until it became a palpable presence.

"Do you feel it?" I asked.

"Oh, wow, yes! I thought it was just me. Even Anxious is jittery. I'm going to use my phone as a torch. I can't stand the dark anymore."

"Good idea. I have plenty of juice in the power bank, so we can recharge the phones if they run low. There should be a light on at the campsite though."

Min lit the way with her phone torch, and it vanquished some of the unease, but not all. It was as though the land itself knew something was wrong and its mistress would never return. After the hard work Leanne had done over the last few years, and now it was for nothing. What a true shame. Just as her business had opened and her future was looking promising, it had been taken away from her.

I resolved to uncover her killer, or help the detectives in any way I could. She deserved justice, even though it was little consolation to her now.

We turned the final bend and sighed as the way ahead was lit by the lights outside the farmhouse and the smart new shower, toilet, and washing-up block. Bright enough to find your way around the site, but not so light it would interfere with anyone's sleep. We hurried to the gate then slipped through and I made sure the latch closed.

We paused at the low stone wall that encircled the front garden. The oak gate was open, swinging back and forth in the wind as it picked up. An almost overpowering scent of Night Scented Stock mocked the sadness, its rich perfume promising a balmy evening and a warm day ahead, but for one person that would never be seen, and it saddened me.

"Leanne always closed the gate, didn't she? She left not long before us to go to the fair, and it was shut then."

"People come and go all the time. She sells firewood and eggs, and gas bottles, all the usual campsite stuff, so one of the guests has probably called but forgot to close it."

"What about her house?" asked Min. "Did she lock up? Would she have bothered? Maybe we should check."

"She wasn't big on security," I said. "Leanne was a chilled woman, and insisted there was no crime up here, and she wanted guests to be able to just walk in and shout hello, although she was always outside fixing things or doing the gardens or mowing the camping fields. You're right, we should check. I wonder if the police will come tonight?"

"Why would they?"

Min stepped into the garden and I followed. Anxious darted ahead to the front door and growled.

We exchanged a concerned look, then I answered her question in a whisper, "Because they'll want to check nothing has happened here. Look for clues. See if they can find a motive."

"What could they find in her house to explain why she was murdered?" Min glanced at the door as Anxious growled again, and I stepped up beside her.

"Who knows? Maybe the place has been ransacked. Maybe the killer came here after she was dead. Maybe they wanted something from inside."

"Then why aren't they here already?"

"I have no idea." I shrugged, then pushed on the door, noting it wasn't even closed properly. It opened with a creak like at the haunted house, although this was for real, not a sound effect.

We looked to each other for guidance but just shrugged. Either we went in or we didn't. The choice was that simple.

"Let me go and check things out. You wait here."

"No way. If there's someone here, we're better off sticking together."

"True," I conceded. "At least let me go first."

Min moved aside and let me enter. Anxious kept on my heels, guarding us unless he was given instructions to investigate.

Min came in behind me and we stood in the narrow entrance that led to the living room on the right or the kitchen to the left. Dark flagstones shone with the age of centuries. Oak so hard and old it was almost black made the interior rather gloomy, but Leanne had installed a modern kitchen with bright plastered walls and the living room was full of modern furniture in oranges and shocking yellows. The incongruous matching of different styles somehow worked perfectly, creating a charming, and utterly unique home for the hardworking campsite owner.

Lamps were lit on side tables and the kitchen spotlights were on above the island and counter, so we entered and paused in the well-crafted room and waited with bated breath, ears straining to catch the slightest sound.

"I can't hear anything, can you?" asked Min.

"No, nothing. Anxious, can you take a look around?" I patted my pocket, the reason never in doubt, so he got busy investigating, nose to the floor, and completed a circuit of the kitchen before checking out the pantry then passed us to search the living room, his claws clacking on the hard floor.

We trailed behind him, eyes never still, looking for anything out of place, but all was as it had seemed when I'd been invited in a few days before to give my details and book my stay. Leanne was slightly scatty, so had piles of papers on a dining table in the spacious living room, with various stacks of books and small projects left in corners or on side tables. She was always fixing something or other, and the renovations were still ongoing, so as well as half re-wired lamps there were machine parts for mowers and even an axe with a new handle waiting to be assembled. I shuddered at the sight of the axe, and wondered if it meant anything or was merely a coincidence.

"Should we check upstairs?" Min whispered in my ear, the warmth of her breath delightful despite my nerves.

"I think so. Um, maybe we need weapons."

"Good idea. Just in case."

We searched the rooms for the most likely weapons, and ended up with a poker each from the fireplace, the huge hearth supported by a thick oak beam above inviting on this cooler evening. Heat still radiated from the stove, a comfort during such a strange time.

The ancient house had a closed door at the bottom of the otherwise hidden stairs, so I opened it, poked my head around to check for homicidal clowns, then breathed and nodded to Min. I went up with her behind me, each tread creaking and making me wince. Anxious waited at the top of the stairs, head angled to the side, questioning why we were being so slow.

The landing light was on, and the bathroom door was ajar, revealing a dated green bath and sink Leanne had joked about possibly keeping because it was so outdated and bizarre it was now retro chic. Two bedroom doors were closed, so with no other choice, I turned the handle on the first, then flung it open and rushed in, poker raised.

Min bustled in behind me, shoving at my back, while Anxious leapt onto the bed with a bright floral throw over the bedding, and way too many cushions piled against the headboard like a tower ready to collapse. Apart from a wardrobe and chest of drawers there was nothing else, so with a nod of encouragement from Min I reluctantly flung open the door and jumped back, relieved to only find Leanne's clothes on metal coat hangers and a simple wooden box on the bottom.

"This is stressing me out," I said, wiping at my forehead.

"You're being very brave. Just one room to go, then we can get some rest. I miss Vee, and can't wait to go home and make a cuppa and sit under the shelter."

"Home?" I asked with a smirk.

"You know what I mean," she huffed, but smiled.

Buoyed by her words, I led the way to the door of the final room. The old metal latch on the oak door was stiff as I lifted it, the clunk loud, the only other sound our breathing. Once again, I shoved the door open and hurried inside, ready to defend my loved ones if an intruder attacked, and almost jumped out of my skin when a woman screamed from the bed and shot upright.

I caught a shocking glimpse of naked breasts before the woman yanked up the covers, her eyes wide with terror.

Anxious barked, then leaped onto the bed, scooted

forward, then collapsed into the terror-stricken woman's lap and wagged merrily before curling up.

"Don't kill me, please. Take what you want, but don't kill me. I'm only young and I don't want to die."

I lowered the poker and said, "I'm not going to hurt you. Who are you? What are you doing here?"

"What do you mean, who am I? Who the hell are you? What do you want? Is this a burglary? Are you going to molest me? Don't molest me, but you can take my phone. I don't have any cash, but take the phone. It's the new iPhone," she confided, eyes darting from me to Min. "Um, why is there a dog on my lap?"

"We're so sorry, " said Min as she lowered her own poker and moved beside me. "We thought there might be a killer on the loose, so came to check."

"A killer? So you are going to murder me?"

"No, another killer. Er, that's not what I meant. There's been a…" Min trailed off, probably thinking what I was thinking, and we both asked, "Who are you?"

"I'm Joy. Leanne's niece."

"Oh, wow, we're so sorry. What are you doing here?"

"I came to visit, a surprise to help out for a few weeks, but she's not here and isn't picking up when I call. I figured I'd get some rest and see her in the morning. It was a long trip and I'm shattered. Hey, did you see my boobs?" she asked, regaining her composure and glaring at me.

Min turned to me and hissed, "Did you ogle this poor girl's lovely breasts?"

I took a moment to consider my answer, then figured it was best to come clean, so admitted, "I saw them, but didn't, er, stare. And I'm not thinking about them now."

"You aren't thinking about my breasts even though we're discussing them?" asked Joy.

"Well, are you?" demanded Min, hands on hips.

Anxious lifted his head, groaned, then hid his eyes

with his paws.

"Traitor," I hissed, before turning to Min and saying, "What am I supposed to say? You're thinking about them too."

"Yes, but only because you ogled."

"I did not ogle! Look, can we please change the subject? Remember why we're here?"

Min's frown was replaced with a sad smile and we faced Joy still sitting in the bed, clearly wondering what these two mad people would do next.

"We're staying at the campsite, and knew your aunt a little. She was a wonderful woman and made us very welcome."

"Why are you talking about her like she's dead?" Joy's eyes wandered from me to Min, then gasped as her hand shot to her mouth. "Has something happened?"

"You haven't heard from the police or your family?" asked Min.

"Why would I? Something has happened, hasn't it?"

"I think we better go downstairs for a chat," said Min. "I'll put the kettle on."

We hurried out of the room and Min slapped my arm then got right up in my face and growled, "Do not think about that lovely young girl's boobs."

I gulped, then promised, "I would never think about such things."

Once Min was satisfied I was no ogler of young ladies, we went downstairs to make a cuppa, ready for the very awkward and heartbreaking conversation that lay ahead.

Chapter 5

I put three mugs of tea and a bowl of sugar on the table in the living-cum-dining room as Joy entered, looking understandably freaked-out but dressed in simple jeans and T-shirt. Her clothes hung loose, a baggy style tee, and she looked like she'd always been slim, not an ounce of fat on her. Thin lips, an aquiline nose, intelligent brown eyes, and a shock of tight black curls on dark skin made me assume she was of mixed heritage.

She paced back and forth before storming over and sitting abruptly, daring us with her eyes to attack.

"Relax," soothed Min. "We honestly aren't here to hurt you. It's as we told you. We knew Leanne."

"What happened?" she sighed, cupping her tea in both hands and sipping, eyes locked on us.

We explained as best we could, and she listened without interrupting, the tears falling into her clutched tea. When we'd finished, she took a big sip, grimaced as it was now cold, then set the mug down.

"Aunty was a wonderful woman. I've been coming every so often ever since I was a kid, and when she inherited this place I helped with the renovations. So did my dad, her brother."

"Any other family?"

"After Grandma died, it's just my dad and Leanne.

Was, I guess. We have loads of family on my mum's side, and most of them are right crazies, but we get on with them well enough."

"But the campsite wasn't left to your dad, but to his sister? How come?"

"Dad got a house in Birmingham in a smart area. Grandma bought it way back when things were affordable. It's run down and is still being renovated. Dad said I could have it to live in as I can't afford rent or a mortgage, but then I had a better idea."

We listened while she gave a potted history of her life.

Joy was twenty-three, fresh-faced, more knowledgeable about the world and the dangers it held than seemed right, and a recent vanlifer. She finished a degree two years ago, found it impossible to get a job that would pay enough to cover even basic rent as everything was too expensive, so lived at home and worked her socks off until she'd finally had enough. With the money she saved, Joy bought a small house on wheels for less than a year's rent of a tiny flat and hit the road. She earned a living via videos she uploaded online to the various platforms, the cash from ad revenue not huge but better than her previous job, and she got to not only live the vanlife but made it her job too.

She explained that the burgeoning vanlife movement had exploded post-COVID, and showed no signs of slowing, which was exactly what I'd heard. It began with her recording her conversion, and the audience grew. People loved getting tips and ideas on how to create their own tiny home, and once she began travelling the fans remained loyal and followed her weekly uploads.

Now she roamed the country to visit beauty spots, but also travelled to out-of-the-way, inhospitable locations as that was what people loved best. Dangerous, wild parts of the country, but never anything too risky.

"That's amazing for someone so young," said Min.

"Thanks. It beats working for a living, that's for sure. It's just an old Ford Transit I live in, but I did a good job with the conversion with Dad's help and it turned out awesome. I love it. Although I always stay in the spare room when I visit here."

"I've got a 67 VW splitty," I explained, and noted the shocked smile with a little smile of my own.

"You're a vanlifer too?"

"It's only been a few months, but yes."

"Max travels all over and is, er, a bit of an expert when it comes to solving strange cases like this," explained Min. "We'll do what we can to help." Min recounted our own past, while Joy listened without comment again. She was definitely a good listener.

"Sounds like we're kindred spirits," she beamed. "What do you enjoy the most about vanlife, Max?"

"The outdoors, I guess. But also the familiarity of knowing wherever I go, wherever I stay, some things never change."

"That's exactly how I feel. I wasn't sure at first, but once I got into it and got to grips with how different life is, I adore it. I'd never go back."

"We can talk more about this tomorrow," I said, "but I'm sure everyone's exhausted. I know I need my bed. Joy, we're going to discover what happened, but we need to know more about Leanne. She didn't seem like someone who made enemies. Is that correct?"

"It is. She was a lovely woman. The best. Never argued with anyone, as far as I'm aware. Never bothered about others, was kind, caring, compassionate, and plain nice. That's no mean feat when life is so tough for everyone."

"Money issues? Debts with dodgy characters? Anything like that?"

"No. She had her own money from selling her place once she inherited here. Not loads, but enough to cover the work she did. I mean, this place had to earn her a living, but she's just opened. Next year was to be the real earner, and now she'll never see it happen." Joy rubbed at red eyes and yawned.

It was contagious, and first Anxious, then Min, then I yawned too.

"Let's call it a day," I said. "The police might call, or maybe you want to phone your dad?"

"I guess I should, yes."

"Shall I stay with you?" asked Min, shifting over and putting a hand to her shoulder.

"No, I'll be fine. Don't worry about me. He'll want to know about his sister, of course, and I'm surprised he hasn't called already. Surely the police notify family straight away?"

"Sometimes they do, sometimes they wait to check a few things out. But maybe they couldn't reach him, and are still trying," I suggested.

"Maybe. But I'll call now."

We said our goodbyes, apologised for the sad news and the shock of us barging into the spare room, then left, closing the door behind us, and waited until we heard the clunk of her turning the key to lock the door.

The campsite was quiet, but still as magical as ever. There was something about this location that went beyond what it appeared to be, and it was hard to pinpoint exactly what that was. Sometimes places felt special and you couldn't really figure out why.

Was it the lights festooned around the various buildings? The way they sparkled and made it feel like Christmas? Possibly. Or how the plots were arranged for privacy but open to the main field? Maybe. The backdrop of rolling hills like something out of a postcard? It certainly helped. There was something else, too, and maybe it was simply the smell. That was it. It just smelled incredible. A mix of the flowers from the garden drifting on the breeze even now, the scent of the pine trees, even the slightly brackish whiff of the lake Leanne had said needed dredging before it could be stocked with fish to attract more business, or maybe just the unmistakable smell of freshly mowed grass.

"This place is so lovely. I can't believe she's gone." Min's words caught in her throat and she sobbed, but then she coughed, dried her eyes, and turned, a determined look in her eyes. "We will solve this."

"We'll do our absolute best," I promised, pulling her in for a hug. "Leanne deserved so much more. This place is special."

"You feel it too?"

"Absolutely." As we headed across the damp grass, Min stopped and chuckled quietly so as not to wake the other few guests.

"What's up?"

"Look at her. At Vee. Isn't she perfect? The little lights twinkling around the sun shelter, the way she sits so low and like she's proud to be our home. It's beautiful."

"You're getting the bug, aren't you?" I teased. "Watch out, it creeps up on you, and before you know it your heart beats faster when you return from the shops and spy her waiting in the car park."

"You're so silly," laughed Min, but when she turned back to Vee and smiled, I knew I was right and she was fast becoming a vanlifer whether she knew it or not.

Another tick in the box for her moving in with me next year, and I had to force myself not to say or do anything dumb, so instead linked my arm through hers and we followed Anxious back to Vee, our spirits lighter than they had been for hours.

"Oh, wow, you did it!" exclaimed Min as I opened Vee and she stepped inside after removing her shoes. This was a new rule, implemented once the weather had changed.

"Yep, I sorted out the Rock n Roll bed before we left. I've forgotten so many times, and then it's hassle doing it right when you're sleepy. The pop-up top is up, too, so there's room for me to move about without looking like a hunchback."

"Then I guess it's time to have a wash, brush our teeth, then bed."

"You can do it here if you like? I usually do now, rather than use the campsite facilities."

"But then you'll have to top up the water supply sooner."

"Yes, but it makes it feel more like home if you get ready for bed here."

"No, I'll go over to the facilities. I need the loo anyway."

"Then I'll come with you."

"Don't be silly. It's only across the field."

"Min, I'm not going to argue, but there's a killer on the loose and although I don't want to scare you, I also don't want you dead. I'm coming."

Min nodded then gathered her things. I figured I may as well take mine, too, so we headed off with Anxious deciding to warm the bed for us rather than hang around outside the toilet block, which showed how smart he was. Five minutes later we were back, and he was fast asleep. I made us a cup of tea so we could unwind for a while even though both of us were flagging, and we sat outside and looked at the stars, neither of us speaking.

Once our teas were drunk, I rinsed out the cups then told Min I'd wait outside while she got ready for bed. Much as I'd insisted the previous night that I didn't mind seeing her getting undressed, she demanded to be allowed her privacy, so I didn't even try to change her mind. She called out once she was in bed, so I entered then closed the door as quietly as I could.

"You'll have to look away," I told her with a grin. "I don't want you getting hot and bothered."

"I'll try my best to tear my eyes away from your trim body," she tittered, but I noted her flushed neck and performed a mental fist pump.

Once in bed, and with Anxious between us, we spoke quietly about our day for a while. It felt good to have somebody to talk to like this, and when we'd shared the same bed yesterday I'd been astonished to find myself in tears when Min had fallen asleep and I listened to her breathing.

It had been so long since we'd been like a married couple, so had hit home when I watched her sleep with tears rolling down my cheeks—this was what I'd been missing. Her too. I'd drifted off eventually and had the best night's sleep ever, and now here we were again.

"What are you smiling at?" she asked, that dreamy, ready for sleep look in her eyes I adored.

"Just thinking how nice it is to be sharing the same bed again. I miss it. I miss you."

"Me too. It's nice having you beside me. And having someone to talk to is a novelty. I'd almost forgotten what it was like."

"It must be harder for you, as at least I have Anxious for company."

"I'm sure you have plenty of deep, meaningful conversations once you guys come to bed," she giggled, both of us watching the little guy twitch in his sleep.

"You'd be surprised," I winked, reaching out and taking her hand.

"Max, do you think Joy's safe?"

"Sure. She locked the house up and I doubt the killer will be after her anyway. There's no certainty, but I'm sure she's fine."

"She's very young, so I hope nothing happens to her. Why would anyone kill Leanne?"

"I don't know. From what I've seen and heard, she was a hard-working, well-respected woman with no enemies. I can't imagine why on earth anyone would kill her, especially how they did."

"You'll figure it out. You always do."
"Let's hope so. Min?"
"Hmm?"
"I'm glad you're here."
"Me too."

She fell asleep soon enough, but I remained awake, and utterly still, not wanting the spell to be broken. I listened to the sound of my two favourites breathing, stifling laughs as they both murmured or twitched, whined or whimpered, and kept Min's hand in mine for as long as I could until she grunted then rolled over to face the wall.

It had been a surprise when she'd said it would be alright for us to share the bed, and that there was no need for me to use the tent. All I could think was that she was becoming more sure by the day about our future, but I knew better than to push it and inquire about anything more intimate. That could wait. It would have to. I didn't want anything to ruin our future together or make her think twice about it. So I trod as carefully as I could, but without being a simpering fool, as who wanted that in a partner?

She knew how I felt, and although I may have reminded her now and then, I also didn't try to be something I wasn't. I did not fawn, simper, or agree with everything she said just because I wanted her back. At least I didn't think I acted that way. I was still me. A man who was at times pig-headed, obsessive, and liked his routines. She knew who I was deep down, and if I'd tried to win her over by acting differently she'd see right through it in a moment, which would lead to nothing but disappointment for us both.

The van was warm, and I grew sleepy despite my desire to savour every moment of this brief return to sharing a bed, and I wondered what it would be like in the winter. I had a small heater, and when I'd tested it the space became insanely hot in minutes despite the lack of insulation, so I was sure it would be snug even in the depths of winter, but what I worried about most was the wet. Maybe I'd invest in a new pair of expensive Wellington boots?

I definitely needed to curb my own enthusiasm for vanlife. Here I was in bed with the woman of my dreams and I was thinking about wellies! I barked a laugh, causing Anxious and Min to groan in their sleep, then closed my eyes and drifted off, feeling truly blessed by being able to share my life with them.

Chapter 6

"Ow! Bugger! Damn! Ugh!"

"Hey, what are you doing?" I asked, rubbing my eyes then stretching out and yawning as I banged my knuckles on the little cupboard door right by my head.

"I was getting the milk for coffee, but I hit my head on the bed. There's no room in here with that thing down. Then I whacked my shin on the table behind the seat, and now I think I've bruised my bum."

"Want me to rub it better?" I grinned.

"In your dreams, mister. Come on, get up. I can't move in here."

"I can't. Anxious is still sleeping." I indicated the still form of everyone's favourite Jack Russell, curled up on Min's pillow, watching me with one eye open, checking if he was going to get a lie-in or not.

"Don't try to pull a fast one on me, you pair. I know your game." Min pouted, put her hands on her hips, cracked her elbow on the counter, and scowled at me.

"We don't know what you mean. Do we, Anxious?"

He trembled slightly, then closed his eyes and began to pretend snore.

"I'm not falling for that!" laughed Min. "Up, both of you. Right now, or there'll be no breakfast," she warned, her tone ominous.

Anxious was up like a shot and out the door faster than you could say yikes.

"Fine. I'll get up too."

My heart sang at the morning camaraderie, and it made me sad in a way as I knew it was just for a few more days then Min would leave. Nevertheless, I jumped out of bed, almost bowling Min over as there was only about a foot of room before the back of the seats. VWs were many things, but spacious they were not.

"What are you doing?" Min screeched, eyes widening in either shock or happiness.

"Getting up?" I shrugged.

"Put some clothes on. You're stark naked. Did you sleep like that all night? Right next to me?"

"Um, yeah. I got hot, so took my boxers off."

"You can't do that."

"No?" I grinned.

"No. Absolutely not. Cover yourself. Have you no shame?"

"Um, not really. It's nothing you haven't seen hundreds, actually, thousands of times before."

"That was different." Min turned away, her shoulders shaking, and I knew she was laughing.

"How so?" I asked, trying to sound innocent.

"We were together. Max, I'm trying to be good and keep this going in the right direction. Don't push things too fast."

"Sorry, and it was a genuine mistake. I forgot I was naked."

"Yeah, right! I won't fall for it."

"Suit yourself. But honestly, I did forget." In truth, I had, but it was a confidence booster to know that Min still got rather flushed at the sight of me in my birthday suit.

I slid on a clean pair of boxers, then my shorts, then

sorted out the bed while Min made coffee in the outdoor kitchen, then joined her.

"Brr, it's a bit nippy this morning."

"Then put a T-shirt on. It's a nice temperature for this time of year. Unseasonably warm. You just haven't got used to it yet. It can't be boiling hot forever. This is proper British weather. None of that crazy hot nonsense that leaves you gasping. I like it."

"Me too, actually. It gives everyone something to talk about." I nodded my thanks as Min passed me a coffee, then sank into my chair and sighed with contentment. "Ah, this is the life. An early start to the day and already we're outside in nature. What a treat that is."

"It is the perfect way to start the day. I know we always used to sit out with our drinks, but it's not the same as stepping out of Vee. It's like we're living right in nature. A real part of it."

"Right?" I agreed. "It's a whole different way of life, and has so much to offer. What I love most is that the cleaning is so easy."

"That's what you love the most?"

"Actually, no. But it's one of the perks. It's this. Being outside rather than cooped up. I know if it's raining or freezing it'll be different, but at least you get incredible views."

"But it's a pain when you want to have a pee, right?" Min smiled smugly.

"Ha, you're trying to make me feel like I need to go, but I woke up a few hours ago and went then."

"You went to the toilet block?"

I mumbled my answer, then studied my coffee.

"What was that? Why are you talking so quietly?"

"I said I went in the hedge."

"You can't do that!"

"Why not? Everyone does," I insisted.

"I don't. And you shouldn't either. It's unhygienic."

"For who? And how?"

"For me. For you. What about the next people who stay here? If everyone peed in the hedge at campsites, the whole place would stink."

"Min, I'm sorry to break the news to you, but everyone does pee against the hedge or behind their tent, or campervan, or caravan, or whatever they're staying in. It's the law of campsites that men are allowed to pee anywhere."

"That is so not a thing." Min gnawed at her lip, then added, "Is it?"

"It is. Everywhere I've stayed, blokes nip off behind their tent, trying to act casual but looking guilty, then return thinking nobody noticed when in truth plenty did. Especially the other men who are thinking about doing the exact same thing."

"I think you're making that up to justify being gross," Min teased.

"Ask Joy then. Here she comes now."

Anxious raced over and greeted his new friend with a hearty bark and an excited wag. Joy laughed as she bent to say good morning, then he trotted beside her as she approached.

"Good morning." Joy smiled, but it was clear she hadn't had the best night's sleep and her eyes were red.

"Morning, Joy. I'm guessing you'd didn't get too much rest?" I asked, standing and indicating she take my seat.

"I got a little, but not too much. I feel like I'm dreaming. Is it really true that my aunty has been murdered with an axe? That can't be right." She sank into the chair with a sigh, nodding her thanks.

"We're so sorry." Min put a hand to Joy's arm and smiled in sympathy.

"Thank you. It felt so weird in the house without her there. I know I was asleep when you, er, woke me," Leanne flushed as she glanced at me and I decided it best not to mention the boobs incident, "but once I knew what had happened I couldn't sleep and roamed around looking at old photos and her bits and pieces. I can't believe she'll never see any of it again. All her hard work and it's for nothing."

"Not for nothing. She did herself and this place proud." I sat on the rug and Anxious hopped onto my lap then lay down after I grabbed my coffee. "Sorry, did you want a drink?"

"I just had one, thanks, and I've been drinking tea all night. I'm waddling rather than walking. I'll probably need another pee soon," she laughed.

"Don't go in the hedge like this degenerate," warned Min.

"Min," I hissed, "you snitch."

"What's this?" asked Joy.

"Max reckons that all men pee in the hedge or behind a tent or vehicle at campsites. I told him it's not true and he should use the proper facilities."

"I do use them most of the time. But now and then, if it's an emergency, I go in the hedge. Everyone does it. It's natural, and doesn't do any harm."

"It kills the grass," tutted Min.

"He's right," said Joy. "I've been living in my van for over a year now, and you see it all the time. Blokes checking if anyone's watching, then hurrying behind their tent for a pee. They think nobody knows what they're doing, but everyone does."

"And do you want people doing that here?" asked Min.

"I honestly don't mind. What's the harm?"

"Ha! In your face, Min," I gloated, grinning then letting my smile fade as now was not the time for joviality. "Sorry, I know that was inappropriate."

"It's honestly lovely to hear you laugh and fool

around. And Min, I'm afraid that if you're going to live the vanlife, it's something you have to get used to. Basically, men are gross!" Joy chuckled, her smile beautiful, and it was so nice to see her trying to be upbeat after such terrible news.

"Who said I'm going to become a vanlifer?" she asked, gnawing at her lip.

"Sorry. I just assumed that you two were…" Joy glanced at us then shook her head and added, "Did I get it wrong?"

"It's complicated," I said, trying to be diplomatic and not put Min on the spot.

"Very." Min brushed a curl from her cheek and smiled at me. "But vanlife does appeal."

It took all my willpower not to whoop and jump up to perform a little dance. "It does? You aren't put off by the cramped conditions, no toilet or shower, or any of the modern conveniences?"

"Of course I am. It's barbaric," she teased. "But I'm coming around to the idea. It's the freedom. Every time I stay in Vee, it's like I'm more connected to nature. It's because you're forced to spend so much time outdoors, and you have to plan ahead and think about what you need and what you don't. It makes you more mindful of everything."

"So true," agreed Joy. "I've found it totally liberating. Not to mention so much cheaper. I do a lot of free sites, and some stealth parking in some incredible spots. I do pay for campsites, too, but that can get expensive. A lot of them have gone up in price lately, so I have to watch my spending."

"You don't miss having a normal home?" asked Min, leaning forward, focus locked on Joy. I was intrigued and excited by her attitude as it boded so well for the future.

"Not really. Sure, some things are hassle, especially in the winter, but it's all part of it. You do things and go places you never would otherwise. More than anything, it's the sense of freedom. This is a beautiful country, and knowing I can go wherever I want does something inside. It truly does give you a different outlook on life and makes you feel part of things, not locked away from it all. Does that make sense?"

"It makes perfect sense," I agreed.

"This is what I'm beginning to understand." Min looked from Joy to me, then lowered her gaze and stared at her coffee.

"Something wrong?" asked Joy.

"No, nothing. It's just… Well, like we said, it's complicated."

We explained about our relationship and it was clearly a shock to Joy, but she didn't ask too many questions, and besides, we had more important things to talk about. Namely, finding out who killed Leanne and why.

I made a second cup of coffee and Joy decided she needed the caffeine, so once we were settled with our drinks Joy said, "I've been going over everything all night, and I can't figure out why anyone would do this. My aunty was the sweetest, kindest woman you're ever likely to meet, so why would anyone kill her?"

"It's a real head-scratcher, that's for sure," I said.

"You said last night that you've been involved in this kind of thing before?"

"Max has solved lots of murders over the last few months," confided Min, beaming at me with pride. "He's got a wiki page all about it."

"Made by my dad, so don't believe all the hype on there."

"Wow, that's cool, I guess. What's the page called?"

Min gave her the address so Joy spent a few minutes reading about my rather embellished exploits, her eyes widening the more she discovered. When she'd finished, she pocketed her phone and asked, "Will you help? Do I need to pay you?"

"Of course we'll help, and no, I wouldn't dream of taking any money off you."

"Phew, that's a relief, because I don't have any," she laughed, trying to hold back the tears. It was no use, though, and her eyes welled before she cupped her face in her hands and wept.

Min consoled her, but it was only when Anxious leapt onto her lap and lifted a paw in sympathy that she managed to regain her composure and dry her tears. She stroked my caring companion absentmindedly as she listened.

"We'll do whatever we can to figure this out," said Min. "Where should we start?"

"I honestly have no idea." Joy sniffed back any more tears and smiled as she looked down at Anxious who groaned then curled up, seemingly happy to remain where he was. "Like I said last night, there were no real money issues, this place is near enough finished so she didn't need to spend much more, and she was so excited to begin taking paying guests."

"It's a lovely site. Simple, but well laid-out, with stunning countryside and yet close to so much too. Perfect." I drained my coffee then figured I should ask the obvious question. "Will you inherit?"

"This place, you mean?"

"Yes. Sorry to ask, but it's important we know. In fact, we need to know everything you can think of about Leanne."

"I think I'll inherit the site and the house. At least, that's what Leanne always said. She knew how much I loved this place. We all do."

"All?" asked Min, eyebrow raised.

"Yes, her, me, and Dad. We always came together for holidays and were always trying to get back here whenever we could."

"What about your mum?" I asked.

"Mum's gone. Passed several years ago."

"Gosh, we're so sorry," said Min.

"We are. You're too young to lose your mum. So you used to visit when your grandmother owned it?"

"Loads of times. She knew we adored it, but Leanne loved it so much and would spend as much time here as possible. It got harder because she had to work, and slowly it fell into decline as it was too much for Grandma, but when Leanne inherited she decided to sell her own house and move here so she could fix it up and start a new career."

"And now it's yours," I said.

"Yes, but I didn't murder her to get it!"

"I'm not saying that, but it's vital we know. What about your dad? Will he be upset that it's yours now?"

"No way. He's happy with the house he got from Grandma, and has a career he loves. He would never live here. Especially because the house he got will be worth a fortune once it's renovated. Dad's got enough money already, and he was so upset."

"You spoke to him?" asked Min.

"Sure, after you left last night. I called him and he was beside himself when he answered. He'd just spoken to the police, a lady detective, and was distraught that they hadn't been able to reach him earlier. He turns his phone off in the evenings when he's watching a show, as people are always trying to get in touch with him."

"What did he say? Anything we should know?"

"Nothing beyond him being so sad and angry, and that he hoped I was handling it okay. He's coming today as soon as he can. I told him not to, but he wouldn't hear of it. He still thinks of me as his little girl, even though I tell him I'm all grown up now."

"Parents do that," I said. "My mum wants me to live back home and never leave the house so nothing bad will happen," I joked, although it was true.

"Dad's like that too. Worries about me being out in

the big, bad world all alone. I can handle myself." Joy's fists bunched before Anxious whimpered in his sleep and she relaxed as she stroked him until he settled.

"Have you spoken to the police?" asked Min.

"Yes, first thing this morning. They called and said that two detectives would be over to talk to me. They should be here soon."

"That's good. We can see if they have any news, and you can tell them what you told us. We met them last night and they're quite quirky, but seem good at their jobs."

"Quirky?" I asked Min. "They were bonkers. Nice, but I kept thinking they were twins even though they were very different ages."

"I thought the same thing! They were nice though."

"Very." I turned to Joy and said, "We promise to help in any way we can. Is there anything you need right now?"

"Just for this to be a dream and for Leanne to holler for me to mow the grass."

Tears fell onto Anxious' fur as he whimpered, picking up on her sadness. It would be a very long day for this young woman, and there was nothing we could do to change what had happened.

Chapter 7

"Here they are now," noted Min with a nod of her head in the direction of the two Susans.

"Who are they?" Joy wiped her eyes and brushed her hair back, her lip quivering, but she was clearly a strong, independent woman and was handling this extremely well.

"It's the detectives. The older, frumpy one is Susie, the younger one with the silver jumpsuit is Sue. They're both called Susan, but figured that would be too confusing."

"You're joking, right? They don't look anything like detectives."

"I know, but looks can be deceiving. Although, the eighties jumpsuit and blue mascara don't make her seem very credible. But trust us, they're nice, and want to help."

"A very good morning to you all," beamed Sue, tugging at the zipper of her jumpsuit and frowning as she inadvertently pulled it right up to her throat before lowering it a little.

"It's a beautiful morning, if quite damp," noted Susie, pulling her grey cardigan tighter across her chest and glancing down at her sensible black slip-on shoes.

We said hello, Anxious sat on Joy's lap, seemingly loathe to leave her, and lifted a paw in greeting followed by a staccato bark to ensure nobody ignored him. He got a hearty greeting and a few head rubs before I made the introductions.

Both the DSs offered their condolences, reminding Joy that they had already spoken on the phone but wanted to get a better picture of Leanne and see if she could shed some light on exactly why she might have been murdered. Joy went over everything she had told us, but there was nothing new to add and the detectives, although friendly, didn't seem too happy with her answers.

"Is there a problem?" asked Joy. "You're acting like I've done something wrong."

"Not a problem as such, but I'm afraid we do have to take a proper statement about your whereabouts yesterday and see if we can prove where you were." Susie glanced at Sue who nodded.

Sue smiled at Joy but then asked, "Can you prove you were on the road at the time of the killing? We don't like to ask, but it will clear you as a suspect. We don't think you did it, but because you believe you'll inherit what is a quite substantial property, we need to go by the book. You understand?"

"Yes, of course, but I promise I would never hurt my aunty."

"Of course you wouldn't," said Susie in a soothing voice. "Would you like a hug?"

"Yes please," gushed Joy. She leaped from her chair, startling Anxious, and flung herself at Susie.

"It's the cardigan," laughed Susie, then wrapped her thin arms around Joy and hugged her tight.

"And the fact you look like an M&S obsessed granny," teased Sue with a loving smile directed at her partner.

"Nothing wrong with that," chuckled Susie as she stroked Joy's head as the young woman sobbed into the detective's chest.

For a few minutes nobody spoke as Joy cried then gradually recovered and took an offered tissue Susie pulled from up her sleeve. Once her face was dry and she'd regained her composure, Joy gave as accurate a description of her previous evening as possible. She'd stopped at a service station about nine, and the DSs assured her that they'd be able to check the CCTV so she should be in the clear.

This seemed to spark something in the two women and they brightened considerably, not that they'd been exactly dour up to this point.

"Now," began Susie, "let's get down to business. What we want to know, is who do you think did it? And why would they kill Leanne in such a terrible manner?"

"I honestly can't think of a single reason. Unless it's simply a case of rivalry between campsites, I can't think of anything."

"People don't kill in such extreme ways just because they don't want the competition," said Sue.

"They don't," agreed Susie, high-fiving Sue and grinning. "What about boyfriends? Was she seeing anyone?"

"Yes, a secret lover, maybe?" Sue's eyes gleamed as she asked the question.

"Nobody that I know of. Aunty had been on her own for a good few years. She said she'd had it with men and was perfectly happy alone. And if there was a secret lover, then that would have been a secret, right? I wouldn't know."

"She's got a point," said Sue.

"She sure has," agreed Susie. "So, if there was no boyfriend, and no love interest at all, what other motive could there have been? You'll inherit, and we trust you, so you're in the clear, but who does that leave us with?"

"The people at the funfair?" Joy suggested, slumping into the chair and gripping the armrests tightly.

"Are you okay?" I asked.

"Just tired. I need to rest soon. This is too much to take in."

"We understand, but just a few more minutes of your time. Why would Leanne have gone alone to the funfair?"

"Because she loved it. We went every year, and that's why I came. But I got here too late and missed out on taking her. She would have been so surprised and pleased to see me, but now we'll never go on the dodgems together ever again. We loved it."

"So she was a real fan of the fair?" asked Susie with a frown, unusual for her as she seemed to be constantly smiling, just like her partner.

"Absolutely. Leanne adored it as much as me. Dad too. And Mum when she was alive. We'd come and stay with Grandma, make a holiday of it and help fix whatever needed fixing here. Sometimes we'd stay for a few days, other times a week or more."

"Did she know the people at the fair?" asked Sue with a knowing nod at a now grinning Susie.

"Great question, Sue," said Susie.

"Thanks," beamed Sue.

"She knew them really well. We all do. Lash is a bit of a grump at times, but he's got a kind heart. It's a hard life they live, and they go through quite a number of employees as people like the romantic notion of travelling and working at the funfair, but the reality is quite different. It's hard work, they have to live in cramped conditions, the days are really long, and it's a very physical job. Assembling the rides and organising things is backbreaking work, but there are a few who have been working there for decades."

"And Leanne knew them well? How so?" asked Susie.

"Because she adored the funfair. She and Dad had been going ever since they were little kids. They used to holiday here. It's how Grandma found this place to buy, and that was after Dad was grown up. She moved here and then everyone had a place to stay when they came on holiday. Leanne loved it here more than Dad, but they both enjoyed the funfair. I guess I took after them and always tried to come every year."

"How well did she know everyone?" I asked.

"Quite well. Enough to chat to and catch up on the gossip. That kind of thing. Why?"

"Tell her, Max," suggested Sue, grinning at me.

"Yes, work your magic," said Susie.

"It's to see if they might have a reason to kill her. Maybe she had an issue with one of them. Anything like that ever happen in the past?" I asked.

"No. They were always really nice to us. Ever since I was tiny, we'd go. Lash would always give me a treat of candy floss or sweets for free, and he'd always ensure we got at least one ride without paying. He was generous like that."

"Think he had the hots for Leanne?" asked Min.

"Oh, he definitely did," laughed Joy. "He asked her out every year, and every year she'd tell him no. It had been going on for so many years it became a running joke. He's not one to give up easily, I'll give him that. He was just fooling around though. It's his way. A rough man, and a real flirt, but he knew she wasn't interested."

"He's a proper carnie type," noted Sue.

"Proper old school, rough around the edges, hard man with a heart of gold," agreed Susie.

"Yes, that's exactly what he's like. A true traveller with a long tradition of never staying in one place. Just like us, Max. Vanlife is pretty new in this country for most of us, but travellers go back generations. A lot of them get a bad reputation because a few people spoil it for everyone else, but the funfair folk are good people."

"We had our eye on him yesterday and he wasn't the most helpful," Sue informed us, "but decided it's just his way. He doesn't really like the police, and he certainly wasn't amused by being shut down and losing out on the takings. They're open today, though, and we've got extra constables on site to ensure nothing else happens." Sue nodded to Susie, who smiled then squeezed the younger woman's hand.

"How can you ensure nothing else happens?" I asked. "Leanne was killed in the haunted house, so how do you patrol something like that? Is it open too?"

"I'm afraid it is. There wasn't much we could do about it. Nobody found anything inside, we have no real suspects beyond Joy here and the unnerving clown, Chuck, but we both agree that the young fellow is innocent."

"He'd have to be daft if it was him, as he was the only other person in the haunted house," said Min.

"I know Chuck," mumbled Joy, her eyes fluttering. "He's a nice boy. Not the sharpest pencil in the case, but sweet. We always get on. He's worked there ever since he left school at fifteen. Not the academic type, but nice enough."

"Then it's settled!" squealed Sue.

"What is?" I asked.

Sue and Susie exchanged a frown then spun sharply to me and both said, "You'll go and investigate."

"Um, you want me to go back there today?"

"Yes please. You too, Min," said Susie. "We want to solve this as soon as possible. The longer this goes on, the less chance there is of discovering the culprit."

"That's how these things work," agreed Sue. "We want Anxious to help too."

"And what about Moose?" asked Min.

"Moose?" Susie shook her head and added, "I'm not following."

"Moose, the security guard you both met yesterday. He joked about maybe you wouldn't remember him even though you both said you'd read about him on Max's wiki page after the trouble at Lydstock."

"I vaguely recall the name," said Susie, a finger to her chin as she thought.

"I've never heard the name before. Are you sure we met him?" asked Sue.

"I'm sure. But it doesn't matter. If it's okay with you, we'll go later today when the fair's open. Once it's lively, there's probably more chance of uncovering something. Maybe the killer will return to gloat," I said.

"That's the spirit," said Susie, beaming at us then her smile fading as her focus turned to Joy whose eyelids were now fluttering constantly. "You should get yourself back to bed. Try to sleep. We'll check with the service station to get your alibi sorted, but don't worry, we won't let whoever did this get away with it."

"Thank you. I'm sorry I couldn't have been more help, but it's too surreal. It's like a dream. I don't know what to do."

"You don't have to do anything," Min told her. "Just rest for now. Your dad will be here later, and I'm sure he can do whatever needs doing." Min turned to the detectives and asked, "Is there anything we can help with?"

"We can deal with Joy's dad for anything that needs attention. But mostly it will be organising the funeral, that sort of thing. We'll pass some details on to him. I assume solicitors will be involved for the will, but that can wait. The main thing is, try to think why anyone would do it. What does puzzle us is why she went into the haunted house alone, and without paying. That's not normal behaviour."

"She always liked to go in there first. Said it got her in the mood for the fair. Without me or Dad with her, she clearly still wanted to enjoy the evening so went alone. I can't imagine her not paying though. I bet Sheena slipped away for a smoke, leaving the kiosk unattended, but didn't want to admit it." Joy shrugged, like it was nothing unusual.

"And Leanne knew everyone there?"

"Yes, but look, they weren't best buddies or anything. She just spoke to them once a year."

"We'll leave you in peace now. Max, let us know if you discover anything. We'll be around, but we have paperwork and other things going on, too, so don't let us down." Susie nodded, so I nodded, too, then the detectives turned smartly and marched off, laughing and chatting excitedly like they were having the best time.

"They're strange," noted Joy once they'd exited the field.

"They're not your average detectives, that's for sure," I agreed.

"I like them." Min smiled in sympathy at Joy, then told her, "Get some rest or you won't be good for anything today. Does anything need doing around here?"

"No, I've already done it. I've been up most of the night so sorted the facilities, stocked up on loo paper and whatnot, so nothing needs to be done. Thanks for the offer though." Joy shook herself out, then stood, and without another word she wandered off, her head bowed, shoulders hunched.

"That poor woman. It's a lot for such a young person to deal with. I hope she'll be alright." Min watched her weave across the field then turned to me. "What should we do first?"

"Breakfast first, then we'll take Anxious for a you-know-what, before going into town for lunch then heading to the funfair this afternoon. Sound okay?"

"That sounds perfect. I know it's awful what happened, but we can't spend all our time trying to figure it out."

"Exactly. This isn't our job, even though I want to help. There's nothing to be done until later, so let's enjoy ourselves as best we can."

"I could do a fry-up!"

A chill ran down my spine and I shuddered, then grunted with relief when Min laughed. "You were teasing?"

"Of course. Remember what happened last time? I couldn't even tell what was bacon and what was sausage."

"The beans were nice, and you did good toast," I

said diplomatically.

"I've finally admitted that when it comes to fry-ups I'm not gifted in the slightest. But what I can do is make some scrambled eggs on toast. Jill gave me her recipe and it's foolproof, so how does that sound?"

"Awesome! I'll go and get cleaned up, and after we eat we can head into town and get supplies for tonight. I want to make a true one-pot wonder, and am looking forward to cooking for just us."

"You did that yesterday, and it was amazing."

"And now I'll do it again. Min, this is a special time for me, so I want it to go well."

"It's special for me, too, and it is going well. We get on better than ever."

"So no bacon," I teased.

"Definitely no bacon."

I gathered my things and used the facilities, feeling better for a shower and brushing my teeth, and truth be told, I was absolutely dying for a pee!

I returned to find Min on her hands and knees, muttering, but kept back to admire the view for a while even though it felt rather naughty to spy on her like this. When she cracked her head on the table as she moved to stand, I hurried forward.

"Are you okay? Why are you crawling around?"

"What? I, er, I wasn't!" Min brushed at her grubby knees then dragged her hair back behind her ears, eyes shifting to the table and the breakfast preparations that were underway.

"Min, you were. I saw you. Why do you look guilty?"

"I'm not guilty. I'm innocent, I tell you. Innocent!"

"Um, okay." I shrugged, then my eyes drifted to the table again and with a smirk I asked, "Where are the eggs? The carton's empty, but they aren't in the pan."

"I, er, I think I lost them."

"You lost the eggs? How is that even a thing?"

"We have another mystery on our hands. It's a real head-scratcher. I swear I was just getting things ready, had a play with Anxious, then they were gone."

We turned our attention to the little guy where he was sitting on the rug, head cocked, studying us.

"Does he look guilty to you?" I asked.

"I don't know. He does that a lot when he's unsure about things. He likes to study us."

"So he can plot, and nick things when our backs are turned," I sniggered.

"But he was inside the van after we played."

"Then where are the eggs?"

"I don't know. Max, this is freaking me out."

"There has to be an explanation. Maybe you put them inside on the counter?"

"I didn't. Someone was here and stole them right from under my nose." Min's eyes darted every which way, then she shuddered.

"I don't think homicidal maniacs steal eggs," I teased with a wink.

"Who knows how they think? We're under attack!"

Min screamed when from out of nowhere an egg landed on her head.

Yolk slid down her cheek as she looked to the sky.

Chapter 8

"What's happening?" wailed Min as she rubbed at her face then began dragging her fingers through yolk and the slimy, gelatinous gunk stuck in her hair.

"It's the missing eggs. Or one of them at least," I chuckled. "No need to freak out."

"It landed on my head! I thought I was being attacked. Where did it come from?"

"There." I pointed to the sky.

"Eggs can't fly. They don't have wings."

"No, but that bird does." I nodded to the tree where a large brown bird took to the wing and was gone before I could identify it. "At least now we've solved one mystery."

"Birds don't steal other eggs, do they?"

"Some do, and I'm guessing it was hungry. It wasn't a magpie, but maybe a bird of prey. It must have been starving, or wanted to use the egg carton as a nest, so was eliminating the competition. But problem solved. Are you alright?"

"Um, I think so. Gosh," chortled Min, "that was quite a shock."

Anxious barked, then whined, and we spun to find that his little head was dripping with yolk and a cracked shell was nestled between his ears.

Unable to stop ourselves, we burst out laughing, the tension released, and Min calmed.

"You poor thing," she cooed, squatting and picking the shell out. "I think we both need to take a shower. Max, do you mind?"

"Of course not. You two get cleaned up and I'll see what I can rustle up for breakfast."

Anxious tried to bolt at the mention of a shower, but Min scooped him up and with his legs still running he whined when he realised he was too late for a great escape. I grabbed the dog shampoo and Min's bits and pieces, then they hurried off, trailing shell and egg in their wake.

I stood, rooted to the spot, trying to find the bird, but it was gone, and our eggs with it. I chuckled, as this was another aspect of vanlife that I adored. Whoever heard of such a thing? Yet it had happened and I was here to witness it. Wouldn't have got that living somewhere more conventional unless we had a home in the country with lots of land, and even then, I got the impression that this was a bird that'd learned that the campsite was easy pickings and had gradually honed its skills. What a wonderful, fascinating world this was we lived in.

Inevitably, my focus returned to the murder and what I could do to help. We needed more time at the funfair, as it was the only place we had a chance of finding anything out. Who kills campsite owners with axes? That was what I had to figure out. Joy was the obvious suspect, but I was sure the DSs would clear her, so who did that leave? Everyone at the funfair, workers and visitors alike, which was a massive pool of suspects.

There had to be a way to narrow it down, but I knew from past experience that the only way to get answers was to go about my business and wait for something to turn up. Lost to my meandering thoughts, it was the screech of a bird that brought me back to my senses, but all I caught was an angry blur of brown as it sailed past overhead then was gone.

I turned back to the kitchen area to see what I could rustle up, and decided to do something simple but a true British staple for breakfast.

"Beans on toast!" I declared, excited by the prospect of a basic but always delicious breakfast, especially when it was sliced white bread instead of anything fancy. You couldn't beat a generous spread of butter on toast then baked beans with added Tabasco and a grind of black pepper.

I nipped into the van and grabbed a tin from the tiny cupboard then hopped out, a spring in my step, and promptly dropped the tin on my foot as I stared at the brown envelope nestled like a surprise gift on my chair. Hopping in pain, I raced as best I could from under the sun shelter and searched, but there was nobody around and I heard nothing.

Cautious, and fretting about Min returning, I snatched up the envelope and unwound the familiar string, the sharp, almost bitter tang of the now worryingly familiar aftershave greeting me as I opened the envelope. This definitely wasn't over, and my stalker had followed me yet again. This time it was different, as Min was here with me, and no way would I let this stand any longer. I had to discover who was after me, and I vowed that I would, no matter what.

Dreading what I'd find inside as there had already been glass, pebbles, and sand, not to mention knives and the smashed window over the last few weeks, I peered inside and found something truly concerning. I upended the contents onto the table and stood back, the metal glistening as the sun slid from behind wispy clouds, bathing the entire campsite in beautiful sunlight. But I felt no warmth, but rather I shivered as I studied the collection of old-fashioned razor blades I hadn't seen or used in years.

Why razor blades? Why any of it? It made no sense, but something had to link these seemingly disparate objects and threats. Pestle and mortar, a knife, sand, stones, glass, and now razor blades. Or was it merely meant to signify metal? Was I finally onto something? Glass, metal, stone, and sand? What did they have in common? Elements? No. Then what? Substances that made other things? Possibly. Dangerous things? Sure, but so were most things in the wrong hands. A link to the murder possibly? Could the razor blades signify the axe used to kill Leanne? Again, possibly, but whoever this was had nothing to do with any of the other murders I'd solved, so I didn't believe they were responsible this time. But maybe they knew about the killing.

Ugh, this was beyond frustrating, and extremely concerning. I had to do something, and soon. What should I do? What could I do? How did I keep Min and Anxious safe? How did I ensure my own safety when someone could sneak up on me like this and I didn't even notice? What concerned me even more was how brazen they were. It would take a...

"No, it can't be," I muttered, shaking my head. Because what I'd thought was that it would take someone with real ninja skills to get so close without me knowing. Could it be Moose? He had the skills, that went without saying, but Moose? It wasn't him; I felt it in my bones. He was a good guy. But if there was one person who had those skills, there could be another. There had to be, because the alternative didn't bear thinking about. I trusted him. He was a friend. Sure, we'd only met a few times, but I liked the guy and surely I wasn't that bad a judge of character?

"I'll have to speak to him and see what he thinks. Time to spill the beans and get him to help," I mumbled, then recalled the beans and retrieved them hurriedly, hating how exposed I felt just bending over.

"What are you muttering about?" asked Min with a perplexed smile, the sweetest sight I had ever seen.

"Nothing. I just dropped the beans. You look stunning. Your hair's wet and shiny in the sun, and your skin's glistening. You look like a model."

"I don't feel like one. Showering with a dog whining and shaking doggie shampoo all over you isn't very glamorous."

"Well, I think you look divine. And you look lovely too, Anxious."

Anxious yipped then wandered off in a huff. Clearly we were both in his bad books for making him suffer so much.

"He's so moody when he gets cleaned," laughed Min, eyes dancing with mirth at his antics.

"He's always been the same. He can jump into a freezing muddy pool, but a nice warm shower in the company of a lovely woman and he gets the hump. I definitely wouldn't grumble about it."

"I bet you wouldn't, but it ain't gonna happen. Hey, what's that?" Min moved to the table and I tried to block her way, but figured I had to come clean.

"Take a seat. I have a few things I need to tell you about. I'm sorry I haven't told you already, but I didn't want to worry you. But it's time you knew everything."

"Max, what's going on?"

"Please, sit down and I'll explain."

Without a word, just a gentle nod of patience and understanding that this was important, Min sat. Anxious took up position beside her, keen to hear what'd been going on too. I guess they both deserved a proper explanation, so I gave them one.

When I'd finished getting them up-to-date, Min surprised me. Rather than looking doleful, possibly scared, or angry that I'd kept such information from her, her jaw clenched, her soft, gentle hands bunched into fists, and she declared, "We'll find out who's doing this. Together."

"You aren't mad? We promised no secrets. I broke that promise."

"I'm not mad. I wish you'd told me, but I understand why you didn't. Max, you were looking out for me." Anxious barked. "Yes, for both of us," she said with a smile.

"Thank you. You, too, Anxious. Together, we'll figure it out. But right now, I have an even better idea." I jumped up, kissed Min on the cheek, fussed with the little guy, then got busy making breakfast.

Ten minutes later, we were as happy as any small family could be. Balancing plates on our laps, sitting in the sunshine, slicing into crispy, well-buttered toast with baked beans that tasted exactly the same as they had since we were kids, and it was lovely.

"You always make such good beans on toast. What's the secret?"

"It's the pepper and Tabasco."

"And the company," she teased.

"Min, I know you're joking, but yes, the company is the most important thing."

We smiled at each other, then tucked in and savoured every mouthful of our simple meal. When we'd finished, I spent a little time cleaning up, arranged the kitchen, fretted over tea towels and cloths as it began to drizzle and I got a forewarning of what was to come when I couldn't hang things out to dry, while Min sorted out things inside Vee. When I went to check on her, I whistled as I studied the interior.

"Wow! It looks better than it ever has. You cleaned everything and put stuff away."

"There wasn't much to tidy as there's no space to make it messy, but I polished the old doors and made the sink sparkle. Now Vee's happy."

"So am I. Thank you."

"No need to say thank you. This is our home, after all."

"Our home," I parroted.

There was an awkward silence as red crept up Min's neck, but she laughed it off in that wonderful way where she forgave herself instantly for any mistake and admitted, "I do think of it as my home, too, now, which I never thought I would. Max, it's so tiny. With the bed down, there's no room at all."

"I know, and a large motorhome would be more practical, but I couldn't do it. Vee feels like part of the family."

"She really does. Whoever thought we'd get attached to a vehicle? And such an outdated one? No air conditioning, no sat nav, not even a CD player let alone a digital radio, and that gearstick is straight out of the Flintstones."

"And you love it, right?"

"I sure do."

Something suddenly dawned on me and I asked, "Would you like to drive today? You haven't driven her yet. Maybe it's time? Break your cherry, so to speak."

"Um, gosh, I hadn't even considered driving. It's your vehicle really. Your dream. I always meet you somewhere, so there hasn't been any need."

"You said it yourself. It's your home too. The number plate reads MAX M1N, which means she's both of ours."

A disgruntled bark made us chuckle, but no sooner had Anxious protested than he curled up on the bench seat.

"Are you sure you don't mind? You won't get all bossy and keep telling me I'm doing it wrong?"

"When have I ever done that?"

"Every time I get behind the wheel. You are the worst passenger ever." She poked me in the tummy and kissed my nose, which I found strangely nice, if very moist and slightly smelling of baked beans.

"Why'd you do that?"

"Because I wanted to!" Min did what can best be described as a terrible dance, bumped her hip on the counter, bounced back and knocked her bum on the rear of the driver's seat, then careened forward into my arms. We fell onto the bench seat, narrowly missing flattening

Anxious, and fell sideways in a heap, laughing, then rolled onto the floor.

We stared into each other's eyes and I could see it coming and knew she could too. Our faces moved closer, Min closed her eyes, and her lips glistened as they puckered.

And then I pulled away and sat on the floor, more stunned than Min by my actions.

"Um, sorry, but I'm being the better man here."

"Wow, that was…"

"Intense? Too close for comfort? A terrible mistake about to happen?"

Min sat up and scooted close, then stared into my eyes as she said, "Not a mistake, no, but I think you saved us both from making things awkward. I'm sorry, I should have known better, and I can't believe you pulled away."

"It's not because I didn't want to, you know, but I know you want to wait. We should. We will. So can you please stop being gorgeous?" I smiled, half of me silently berating myself for stopping things going too far, the other half annoyed I was an idiot for refusing her.

"I get it, and thank you. It's this cursed van. She's doing it on purpose."

"You think Vee's trying to get us back together before next summer like we decided?"

"I do. But we have to wait. You hear me, Vee?"

The horn beeped, making us both jump then stare at each other in astonishment.

"No way! She's turned into Herbie," I whispered.

"Incredible. She's sentient?"

Agog, we crawled forward and peered over the driver's seat only to find Anxious there with his paw up, a dastardly grin on his face.

Min cradled the prankster, then rolled back onto the van floor and we laughed until it hurt, then laughed some more. I think it was one of the best moments of my life. It brought not only hope, but certainty, and I felt a deep love for all of them, Vee included.

When we'd finally tired of our sides hurting and getting stomped on or licked, sometimes both simultaneously by Anxious, we jumped outside and into the sunshine. Something had changed; we all felt it.

"We're a proper family," said Min.

"That's what I felt too. Together, if only briefly, but that doesn't matter. We'll always be together. Now, are you going to drive?"

"If you're sure? I don't want to break the campervan." Min gnawed at her lip as she glanced at Vee, her two-tone orange and white paint job sparkling as if she couldn't wait to show Min how unpredictable a vehicle she was to drive.

"I'm sure. Just watch out for third gear, don't press too hard on the brake or you'll tear her in half, you might want to hold on to the door handle when you go around bends as the door has a habit of opening, and if you hit a pothole, be sure to crack your spine back into position."

"Anything else?" she asked with a pout.

"Oh yeah, loads more," I said happily. "And you're about to find out."

Chapter 9

"It's okay, buddy. She didn't mean it, did you, Min?" I held Anxious tighter, his small body trembling as he looked from her to me, adoration and trust in his eyes. Plus, fear. I was sure I had the same look.

Anxious whimpered and snuggled into my shirt, his wet nose making me start as it poked my belly.

"Of course I didn't mean it!" Min gripped the large steering wheel tight and frowned. "There's no power steering. How am I meant to turn the corners? It's like wrangling with a cow that wants to go in the opposite direction."

"How many cows have you wrangled?" I stifled a laugh then squealed as the campervan brushed the hedge, a stone wall up ahead making me fear for our safety and the future of Vee.

"None, but it can't be harder than this." Min grunted as she slowed, pressing too hard on the brakes and causing our seat belts to snap taut. She heaved and managed to take the bend, but instantly hit a pothole. The whole undercarriage protested along with my spine. Anxious burrowed deeper until he was more under my shirt than on it.

"You hit a pothole," I said helpfully.

Min's head snapped around, ready to do something

she seldom did and let loose with a tirade of cursing, but when she saw my smile her features softened and she laughed. "You aren't mad?"

"Mad? Of course not. Terrified, hurting, and worried about my bank balance, but not mad."

"I thought you'd be giving me grief the whole time."

"You're doing great."

"I am not! I'm awful. I can't control Vee properly and the brake is so sensitive one minute then doesn't hardly work the next. Is that right?"

"It's an old vehicle. It's had plenty of repairs and new parts, but it's how these campers are. And besides, you're doing better than I did when I first got her."

"I find that hard to believe."

"It's true. There's a real knack to driving her, and it took me ages to figure things out. It's why I've been warning you about so many things. Not to make your life harder, but so you know to watch out for it. Oh, if it rains and you need the wipers, ignore the numbers on the lever. You have to do the opposite, and it's down not up. The lights are flaky, too, so you need dipped headlights, and the full beam is so bright you have to ensure you turn it off before anyone comes towards you."

"Anything else?"

"Loads," I said merrily, enjoying myself despite the discomfort and fear.

Min wrangled with Vee for the next ten minutes, then we arrived in town. She sighed as we were caught in traffic and had no choice but to take things slowly, then pulled off into a car park and suddenly stopped and turned to me, eyes wide and sweat beading on her forehead.

"What's wrong? Did you see someone?" I checked outside but saw nothing unusual.

"I can't park it! How am I supposed to reverse in? I'm not used to a large vehicle, especially without power steering."

"You'll do fine. Take it slow, be sure to use your mirrors, and let Vee guide you in."

Min did a double take then snorted, "Are you serious? She isn't hands free."

"Up to you," I shrugged. "I can do it if you want. I was terrible at reversing, so practised. Just have a go."

"I will." Min squared her shoulders, pulled past the parking spot and across the road, then checked her mirror and tugged on the wheel like she was steering a ship back in the day then crunched into reverse, causing us both to wince and Anxious to whine.

Suddenly, she hit the accelerator, spun the steering wheel frantically, then slammed on the brakes, killed the engine, and turned and said, "Perfect," grinning broadly.

"Brilliant! You got me beat. Even now, it often takes me a few tries."

"Thanks. That wasn't so bad." Min tapped the steering wheel and said, "Thanks, Vee."

We waited, but there was no beeping of the horn, just the ticking of the air-cooled engine gradually recovering.

We gathered what we needed, namely, one dog and two bags, then found the high street and did a spot of shopping. The funfair was closed here, but we both assumed it would be open, especially outside the town hall, by the afternoon. We picked up some choice ingredients for lunch and dinner, perused the boutique clothes shops because Min wanted to and I got the chance to hang outside with Anxious and chill, then found an awesome deli. With a mouthwatering selection of meats and cheeses, quiches and cakes, we blew a ton of cash on a picnic lunch despite what we'd already bought, then wandered around a little more—it was time for lunch before we knew it.

"How did we spend so long shopping?" I wondered. "I'm hungry, but it feels like we just had breakfast."

"It's a larger town than I realised, and we took ages in the deli."

"And a few minutes in the clothes shops too," I added diplomatically.

"Yes, maybe a few," said Min with a wink. "But I got you a nice shirt and found a lovely dress for me. What a fabulous morning. We'll have to come back later to get a few more things, and I want to check out that place with all the buckets."

"You do love a bucket," I sniggered. "But I want to go there, too, to pick up a few cloths and whatnot."

"Thank you for letting me drive. I know Vee means a lot to you, so I appreciate it."

"I already told you, she's for both of us. I don't want you to feel left out. Now, let's go find a nice spot and have our picnic."

With Anxious sniffing at the bag like a bloodhound on the trail of a missing felon, we hurried along the street then followed the signs for a park containing a botanical garden, a play area, and a river. We found it soon enough and strolled along the river, soaking up the atmosphere on what was turning out to be a pleasant, dry day with plenty of sunshine of the more usual British variety. Boiling, then cloudy, then cool, then sunny again. Exactly what we were used to.

We smiled at people out for a stroll, walking dogs, or riding bikes, and plenty more who seemed to be rushing back to work or in a hurry to get to the shops to buy lunch before they were left with a manky flattened sausage roll or a stale sandwich. Min spotted a bench beside the riverbank, so we sat gratefully. Anxious hopped up into the middle, then we began unwrapping everything and laying it out as best we could without him snaffling the lot.

Each of us had our fill of the picnic, taking our time, which didn't go down too well with the bottomless pit named Anxious, but he behaved impeccably and didn't steal anything, at least not that I saw. Once we'd finished, without overdoing it, we packed the rest up and I returned everything to the cool bag I'd brought to keep our produce fresh until we got back to the van.

"Let's go up the hill and sit on the grass," I suggested. "Anxious can run around, we can chill out, and then we'll load things into the van and visit the funfair. Sound good?"

"Sounds perfect. It's so nice here by the water, and look at the swans. They're such an amazing bird."

We sat for a while longer and admired their grace and beauty as they glided across the meandering river, their arced necks an astonishing thing to behold. Reluctantly, but with Anxious keening for some exercise, we took the path up the rise then made ourselves comfortable and Min told Anxious he could go and play, but not to roam too far. With a yip of excitement, he tore off and raced around the field, dodging kids playing football and sniffing various dogs until he found someone who wanted to play. We spent fifteen minutes laughing and smiling as he tore around with his new buddy until the dog was called by its owner and had to leave.

Anxious came back slowly, tongue lolling and as happy as always. I gave him some water from the collapsible bowl I always carried, then he lay on his side, panting, and was asleep in minutes.

"Look, isn't that Lash with one of the lads from the fair? Gaz, I think it was. Chuck the clown said Gaz worked with him in the haunted house after nine when he finishes working on the rides. He seemed to like him."

"They don't seem very happy with each other. Looks like they've been shopping."

"Why are they carting so many shopping bags around? You'd think they'd park at a supermarket to shop, not lug the bags all over town."

"Max, not everyone goes to the supermarket. We didn't. We wanted to shop locally to support independent businesses, and you can't get what we bought in Tesco or Sainsbury's, not even Marks and Spencer. See, they have some of the same bags as us."

It was a stretch to read the bags, but Min was correct. I could just make out the logo for the deli on several. "I guess Lash likes the finer things in life. You'd think he'd be strapped for cash."

"Why would you think that?"

"You're right. I'm being judgemental. I guess because of the way he dresses and his demeanour, I already had him as a cheapskate. He was more stressed about losing earnings than the death, which now I think about it is even more odd considering how he knew Leanne and propositioned her every year."

"I bet he hardly even remembered her. Think how many places they go to every year. He probably does it to a handful of women in every town. Look, they're getting angrier with each other now."

It was an incongruous sight. Gaz was dressed in full zombie costume. Presumably he'd already been working on the rides and had to remain dressed up all day and night, and yesterday I'd noted several others in various costumes. But seeing a zombie in tattered clothes and heavy makeup so his eyes looked sunken and his teeth blackened, shaking his fist at Lash was beyond peculiar.

"I hope he doesn't bite him," laughed Min.

"Whoa! That's a bit much." Lash had grabbed Gaz by his ripped chequered shirt and pulled him close to his face until their noses almost touched. He was shouting loud enough for us to hear, but not catch the words. Gaz dropped his bags and shoved at Lash who released the younger, much smaller man and stepped back then wiped his head.

"Should we do something?"

"I think they're cooling off."

Lash pointed at the bags, snapped a few curt words, then turned on his heels and marched off. Gaz snatched up the bags and chased after his boss, but remained behind until they were lost down a side street.

"At least we know they aren't always one big, happy

family," noted Min with a sigh and a shake of her head. "That's no way to treat an employee though. He could get into trouble for being so violent."

"They aren't exactly a conventional business, and I bet tempers run high when you're living on top of each other and work such long hours. But you're right, he shouldn't put his hands on him like that."

"How old is Gaz?"

"Not sure. Early twenties maybe? A little older than Chuck but much younger than Lash. Why?"

"Just wondered. Maybe they're related."

"Nobody mentioned anything about them being family, but they could be father and son, I suppose. Doubtful, though, or it would have been noted. Any more pork pie left?" I glanced at the bags, salivating at the thought of a few more nibbles.

"We ate it all. There's still quiche, and those olives with the peppers inside if you want?"

"I shouldn't. We ate loads."

"True."

For a moment we just stared at each other, then laughed, as who were we kidding?

We tore into the cool bag and treated ourselves to a few choice morsels, plus a little for Anxious, then decided we'd better leave before we ate the lot and were too full to move. It was a short trip back to the camper where I managed to get the perishables in the tiny gas-powered fridge. It was still the one thing I wished I could change, as for a man obsessed with food and who always wanted fresh ingredients it could have been three times the size and still not big enough.

Min was sitting on a camping chair on the grass beside the car park, looking smug, so I joined her and she handed me a cuppa, eyes twinkling.

"What are you looking so pleased about?" I asked, stretching out my legs.

"Max, we just did the shopping, and now we're relaxing in our own chairs, drinking coffee I made, but we haven't had to go home because our home is with us. It's so cool."

"But we are next to a car park," I noted.

"Who cares? We're off to the fair next, then back to the campsite for a stunning dinner. It's perfect. Even the sun has come out to cheer us on."

"True, and it's turning into a fantastic day. Not toasty, but warm enough for September. This is the life, eh? Watching people come and go, knowing we can go anywhere, do anything. And as far as car parks go, it's not too bad."

Min sighed as she sipped her coffee, then gasped and said, "Wow, look at that VW. Very cool. It's matt black. Not as old as yours, I don't think, but very smart. Even the wheel rims are black."

"Since when did you have an interest in wheel rims?" I teased.

"I like wheels," she countered with a cheeky wink.

My eyes drifted from her to the car park, and it suddenly clicked whose van it was. If not, it would be even more of a coincidence than it already was.

"I think that's Dubman's campervan. Remember I told you about him? The guy at St Davids who I kept bumping into?"

"The one who sorted out the party on the beach then helped you get the killer to reveal themselves? That guy?" Min frowned and her leg began to bounce up and down as she was clearly concerned.

"Yes. What's wrong?"

"Max, this is a crazy coincidence, don't you think? You said you kept bumping into him at St Davids and now he's here? What if he's your stalker?"

"Dubman? No way."

"You aren't thinking clearly. Come on. If this was

anyone else's case, you'd be instantly on the alert and thinking it was him. He's following you. He was around all the time in Wales, and your stalker had to be watching your every move. It's this Dubman guy."

"I understand what you're saying, but he doesn't give off that vibe. He's too like me, I guess. Although, not as handsome." I offered Min my best cheesy smile and she batted my arm playfully, but soon turned serious again.

"Max, you need to think about this logically. Who is the ideal match to be your stalker?" Min held her hand up to stop me answering. "No, don't say anything, just think. Who will blend in, can travel at a moment's notice, is used to this life, and knows more about it than anyone else? A fellow vanlifer, that's who. Not someone from your past life in the kitchens, but someone who lives how you live and nobody would give a second thought to because campervans are so common these days. You aren't looking at this logically."

"Sometimes logic doesn't come into it."

"Really?" Min raised an eyebrow.

"Yes. I know that sounds like an excuse, but it really isn't. Min, you know I get a feeling about people. I'm not always right, granted, but Dubman doesn't fit the profile."

"You've profiled your stalker?"

"Um, well, no, I haven't actually," I admitted, beginning to feel foolish for not even seriously considering Dubman, but then I tried to explain. "I'm not sure how to put this, but sometimes you just know something, right? Like with Leanne's killer. There's something we need to uncover that will explain why she was murdered in such a horrible way."

"We can agree on that."

"And it's the same with whoever is doing this to me. There's obviously a reason. There always is. That goes without saying, I know, but what I'm getting at is that he isn't the type and doesn't fit with what I imagine my stalker's background is. Dubman is from St Davids and has been a lifer for a year or so. Before that, it's doubtful our paths would have ever crossed."

"But you might have had an issue with a friend of his or a member of his family, or he might have worked for you in a restaurant and looked different. It could be anything."

"I know, but it still isn't Dubman."

"Did someone mention my name?" Dubman smiled down at us as he brushed a long brown lock from his tanned face.

Anxious barked a greeting and wagged.

That meant I was definitely right about this mysterious man. Didn't it?

Chapter 10

"Eek!" Min slapped a hand to her mouth, but I merely grinned as Dubman frowned then shrugged before squatting to fuss over the little guy who instantly hopped onto his legs and flopped over for a tummy rub.

"See," I gloated, nodding to the pair.

"Wow, Anxious, good to see you, too, buddy. It's been a while."

"Not long really. How are you doing?" I asked, happy to see the man I classed as a friend.

"All good, mate. Been trying to make the most of the weather before it turns nasty. It's no heatwave, but it'll do. I'm riding the wave of shorts and sandals until the very end, but it won't be long before we'll be huddled in our vans with the heater on and dreaming of summer."

"It's going to be a challenge. How did you cope last winter? That was your first one, wasn't it?"

"Sure was, and it came as a shock to the system. Old VWs weren't built like the modern ones. There's no insulation, and it can get pretty nippy, but with a few tricks it worked out okay. Main thing was the washing. But any excuse to use the launderette, as they're always warm." Dubman laughed, then lowered Anxious who wandered back to Min and barked at her, as if saying that it was alright and Dubman was our friend.

Min stroked him but remained silent, eyes hooded as she sized up the man before us clad in three-quarter length green cargo shorts, a tight T-shirt, leather sandals, and with a tan as deep as mine. He was shorter than my six one, maybe five ten, and stocky, but with hair like mine, a friendly, open face, and high cheekbones, he was undoubtedly handsome.

"I do love a launderette," I sighed, thinking of the toasty times I'd had in the numerous ones I'd whiled away a few hours in, taking a nap or just watching the drums go around and around. "Oh, Dubman, this is Min, my ex-wife and best friend besides Anxious. Min, this is Dubman."

"Nice to meet you," said Dubman with a smile that slowly faded as he put his hand out to shake and Min hesitated before extending her own hand cautiously.

"You too. Sorry, you must think I'm so rude, but we were just talking about you."

"All good things, I hope?" he asked, raising an eyebrow at me.

"Actually, no," I reluctantly admitted.

"No?"

"Remember I told you about my stalker?"

"You did?" asked Min, shocked.

"Sure, man, it sounded nasty. Having more problems?"

"I am, and when I told Min I was sure the van was yours, she said it's most likely you who's after me."

Dubman dropped to the grass casually, and sat with his legs crossed, facing us. He rubbed at his short beard for a while, making me stroke my own much longer facial hair, then he said, "I understand. You're worried about Max, as whoever is following and threatening him is clearly unstable. Now I turn up and we kept bumping into each other at St Davids, so I get where you're coming from. Min, there's no need to be concerned. I swear it isn't me. I'm a good guy, I promise."

"Min, what do you think?" I asked.

"You've put me on the spot," she squirmed, "but I think you might be right. If you're a friend of Max's, and Anxious', then I guess you must be a decent bloke. I'm so sorry for being rude. It isn't like me."

"Don't sweat it. You're looking after your fella, right?" he chuckled, winking at me.

"I suppose I am. I'm not normally so rude, though, but this has got me very rattled. Max takes everything in his stride, but this is serious. Today it was razor blades."

"I think you better tell me everything."

We explained what had been going on since we arrived, including the murder, a little about Leanne, even her niece, and then about the razor blades. Dubman, aka Roger, listened attentively and asked a few pertinent questions. Once we'd finished, he leaned back and thought for a while, before admitting with a short laugh, "It's got me stumped. Either you did something nasty to someone back in the day, or they think you did. As for the murder, well, that's your thing, mate, not mine. I stay away from anything too serious like that as it puts a real downer on my vibe, but it's your calling. I checked you out after you left, read your wiki page, and you've got the gift for sure. Use your skills to uncover the truth. If you need any help, just holler."

"Thanks. I appreciate it. Let's exchange numbers, and maybe we'll bump into each other. You could always meet us at the fair later, or come over for dinner. I was going to invite Moose this evening, Min and I already agreed, so you're more than welcome."

"I got things planned for today, but thanks for the offer. But tonight would be good. You can fill me in on the rest then."

"That would be great."

We swapped numbers, then he said goodbye and left in his campervan; neither Min nor I spoke until he exited the car park.

"What do you think now?" I asked.

"I'm amazed you shared so much with a total stranger."

"Me too. It's not like me to be so open with anyone I don't know. When we first met, I basically told him everything that had been going on. He seemed so genuine, and I just talked without even considering what I was doing."

"Then he can be trusted. Anxious likes him, and he's a great judge of character. Sorry again for being so awkward about it. I'm just concerned about you."

"I understand, and thank you for caring."

We packed our things away in our home on wheels, then Min made the short drive to the funfair where she parallel parked without any issues and beamed at me as she turned off the engine. "Driving for the second time felt better. More familiar. We should have walked, but I wanted to practice again. I think I'm getting the hang of it."

"You're a natural. It means I can put my feet up and doze while you drive us around the country."

"Hey, it's only for today. And if you think I'm doing all the driving, think again. And besides, I know you, and you're itching to drive Vee, aren't you?"

"You know me too well," I laughed, then leaned over and kissed Min on the cheek.

"What was that for?" she asked with a smile, rubbing at her face. "And you need to cut that beard. It's getting dangerous."

"It was to say thank you for being so understanding, and for having my back."

"Always." With a tug at my beard, and a high-pitched giggle, Min hopped out of the camper and I chased after her, Anxious on my heels, barking excitedly and happy to play along with whatever this game was. I caught up with Min and swept her off her feet then twirled her, before letting her down gently and we stood there, holding hands but at arms' length, grinning, neither of us knowing quite why.

"What's got into us?" asked Min.

"We're enjoying ourselves, but for some reason I feel really wired."

"Me too. Must be the caffeine. Now it's time to get serious though. We need to do our best to question everyone today without it seeming weird or annoying them. Maybe we should go on everything as that way we can talk to staff manning the booths or rides and get a better idea of what everyone thinks of what happened and who they believe could do it."

"Great idea. You do the scary stuff, I'll hang out on the dodgems then see if I can snag a rubber duck with a hook before I try my luck at knocking a stack of cans over with a ball."

"No chance! You have to come on some of the rides with me."

"Just the gentle ones. Nothing that will make me ill. Maybe we shouldn't have had our picnic."

"We'll be fine. And by the sound of things, the funfair is up and running and, if anything, louder than ever."

"You're right, and it's only the afternoon. Think what it'll be like tonight. I guess it hasn't put people off coming."

And boy was I right. As we approached the outskirts of the funfair, it was evident that the place was busier than the previous day. Kids were screaming as they rode suitable rides, adults were snapping photos and queuing at the more intense ones, and the closer we got to the town hall and the heart of things, the more crowded it became.

The going was easier here, though, as the rides were more spread out and everyone had more room to breathe. Plenty of visitors were set up on blankets, enjoying picnics and drinks, with numerous bottles of wine present. It was a true festival atmosphere.

"Why is it so rammed?" I asked Min as we moved

away from the densest area so we could actually take in the number of people properly.

"It's the first full day, isn't it? Yesterday was just for the evening, so I guess everyone's come to enjoy themselves. It's Saturday, so people aren't working. And don't forget, this is the biggest and best funfair in the whole country." Min couldn't contain her smile as her eyes roamed from the people to the rides, trying, and failing, to take it all in.

The noise would have done any music festival proud too. Along with the endless stream of announcements for rides about to begin, music blared from speakers, but even that was almost drowned out by the hubbub of the visitors. Everyone seemed hyped, almost manic, and I wondered if the energy was contagious and that was why we were wired after leaving Vee.

Once we'd got our bearings and settled into things, we decided to make our way to the haunted house and see what had developed there, maybe catch up with Sheena who should be working the ticket kiosk that served several other rides too. I couldn't imagine that the haunted house would be open, but she should still be stationed there. I was also hoping to catch up with Chuck, but wasn't sure where he'd be.

I was also beyond keen to find Moose and see what he'd uncovered, and share our news about Joy and see if he'd heard anything. Anxious wasn't too impressed with the volume of people, or the crackling speakers, but squared his shoulders and shook his head when I offered to carry him, so we headed to the side of the field where it was quiet, then skirted around the edge towards the haunted house where we assumed the crowds would be thin and the noise levels much lower.

How wrong we were. As we approached, the noise intensified, and soon we found ourselves stationary and in a line.

"Why are they queuing?" asked Min with a frown as she turned to me. "No, it can't be, surely? They wouldn't, would they?"

"I think they would. In fact, I'm positive they have."

As the line progressed, it became clear from the chatter that our worst fears were confirmed. We soon got to the ticket booth where Sheena was sitting behind the plexiglass, a new sign tacked over the price, the cost doubled. It clearly wasn't stopping anyone from buying tickets, and for only one thing.

"This is in bad taste, isn't it?" Min asked Sheena.

"You're telling me," she sighed, flicking a limp strand of hair from her red face. "I'm boiling in here as I haven't had the chance to take a break yet. It's been non-stop ever since we opened hours ago. Everyone wants to see. It's pretty sick if you ask me."

"But you're still doing it. Serving tickets, I mean," I noted.

"Don't you dare judge me! This is my job, and Lash doesn't take kindly to anyone disobeying him. It's his business and he can run it as he sees fit. But I ain't too pleased about it, I can assure you." Sheena's face crumpled like old parchment as she sneered, her thin lips pressed down in a pout, but her eyes were determined and she clearly wasn't happy with me for asking, or Lash for insisting.

"I'm not judging. I'm saying everyone has options."

"That's fine coming from someone with plenty of cash and a nice place to rest their head," she growled, shifting forward on her stool until her face touched the screen dividing us. "But for us folk who live paycheque to paycheque, we don't have that luxury. Don't you dare look down on me."

"Sheena, you've got it all wrong. I'm not looking down on you. All I'm saying is I'm sure Lash would understand if you weren't up to it. Did you ask to change jobs for a day or two?"

"No, because this is my spot and I'll be damned if I'm going to lose it because some nutter decided to kill a punter. Are we clear?"

"As crystal," I said with a grin, trying to show that I wasn't angry or judging, but failing as she just scowled.

"Do you want tickets or not?"

"Of course we don't want tickets! We promised to help figure this out, but we don't need to go inside again. Have you heard anything? Any talk last night about who it might have been? Or anything else that happened?"

"Just fools spouting nonsense. Everyone was upset, of course, and so they should be, but let's get real here."

"Yes?" we both asked.

"The staff are more worried about being accused than that someone died. Only a few of us knew Leanne. And yes, I know I acted like I'd never heard of her when I first met you guys, but I didn't want any trouble. The rest have never heard of her, but they know what the public can be like. Cruel, accusatory, quick to judge, and everyone is expecting trouble today. It won't happen yet, but come this evening there will be bother, I guarantee it."

"What makes you say that?" asked Min.

"Because we're fairground folk and have a bad reputation. People think we're the ones who cause trouble, make a mess, disrupt towns we visit, but we're good people, same as most others. Mark my words, once it's dark this place will be like a war zone. Groups of lads with too much ale in them, full of bravado as they're with their mates, and they'll try to take it out on us."

"I hope it doesn't come to that," I said. "Look after yourself and try to keep a low profile."

"If I can, I will, but I'm stuck here all day and evening with just a few breaks. I need a career change," she grumbled, reaching to the side and grabbing a grubby cloth then wiping her sweaty face, her oily skin and missing teeth making her look frightening.

People behind us began to grumble and call for us to hurry up, so we shifted aside, skirting the queue ahead now waiting to get inside, the door controlled by a member of staff we hadn't seen before. We stood watching the eager faces, everyone chatting in groups they came with about how exciting it was and that they were going to go inside a real murder spot, seemingly unconcerned about their own safety.

"These people are nuts," whispered Min. "It's pretty twisted."

"People have always had an interest in crime scenes, and this one is quite outlandish. A real murder in a haunted house manned by clowns and zombies and at a funfair. It's the perfect spot to drum up interest. Think about all the old murders from years ago and how people flock to the sites to look at where they happened. Now they can come the very next day and take photos and upload them. It's the way things are now."

"I don't like it. It's disrespectful to Leanne."

"But they didn't know her, so it doesn't mean the same to them. It isn't personal. It's just exciting. The place must be taking so much money, especially with the price hike."

"There's more to life than money," said Min a little too loudly, causing heads to turn before they ignored us and shuffled forward.

"Hey, there's Moose. Let's go have a chat." I pointed to the dodgems where he was standing on the metal platform surrounding the area with the cars, so we turned away from the strange scene and went to see what news he had. We only managed a step before I bumped into someone, and as I apologised, Joy appeared from behind him, looking tired but smiling.

"Max, this is my dad, Rupert."

"Hi," I said with a smile. "Sorry to bump into you."

"It's hard not to with this crowd," he said with a frown and a raised eyebrow to his daughter.

"Dad, this is Max, and this is Min. They're the people I told you about."

"The ones ogling my daughter in her bed?" he

asked, fixing his eyes on me.

"That was a misunderstanding," said Min, extending a hand and beaming.

"I already told him that. Dad wanted to come down to the fair and see things for himself, and we just came from the haunted house. It's awful what they're doing."

"Utterly disrespectful," tutted Rupert. Unlike his daughter, he was a very prim and proper looking man with a pale pink shirt buttoned to his neck and a grey waistcoat. Dark chinos and sensible shoes completed the ensemble. Short red hair parted at the side made him rather hard to remember, as there was nothing distinguishing about him.

"We didn't like it either. We spoke to Sheena at the kiosk and she agreed it was in bad taste, but Lash decided to try to claw back some of the lost revenue."

"When I find that man I'll give him a few choice words, but I can't stand it any more. We're leaving."

Anxious barked, clearly miffed at being ignored, so Joy introduced her father to him and both seemed to relax as they gave him an ego boost by commenting on his fine fur and clean teeth. Rupert explained that they used to live with a Jack Russel when he was a lad, so had a real soft spot for the breed.

"Don't get too angry with Lash, Dad," pleaded Joy as Rupert stood and searched the crowd, clearly intending to have a few words.

"I will tell him exactly what I think of this. My sister is dead and he's making money from it." With a nod, he marched off, leaving Joy in a quandary and clearly unsure what to do.

"I better go after him. He's so upset about Leanne, and this has made it worse. See you guys later?"

"We'll see you back at the campsite," said Min with a sympathetic smile.

A young man, eyes glued to his phone, and smoking a cigarette, bumped into Joy.

"Hey, watch it!" she warned, scowling at not him but his dangling cigarette. "And put that out. It's gross."

The man sneered, then threw his half-finished smoke to the ground, fished out another, and lit it.

Joy blanched and took a step away, wafting the smoke from her face, and slapped the cigarette from his mouth. He gaped, then took one look at me and simply ambled off, muttering.

Joy smiled weakly and said, "Sorry about that, but I hate smoking. He should know better," then hurried after her father.

We went to chat with Moose.

Chapter 11

Just like the rest of the fairground, the dodgems were busy, with people waiting their turn, the little tokens that you slotted into the dodgems clutched tightly in their hands or standing impatiently in the long queue at the booth, waiting to be served.

Moose had his back to the cars and was scanning the crowds, eyes constantly roaming. We stopped and watched for a while, and I marvelled at how people seemed to flow around him as though he were a static structure, part of the building almost. Nobody noticed him at all, even considering his size, rather they skirted around, their chatter ceasing until they were past, not knowing why but behaving differently, calmer and quieter, then shaking their heads and chatting and smiling again like nothing had happened. It was uncanny and impressive, and utterly perplexing. Was it only us that could see him?

"People think he's a girder," said Min, voice full of wonder. "It's like they don't see a person at all. He'd be an incredible thief. Or murderer," she said ominously.

"Hey, that's our friend you're talking about."

"I know, but I'm just saying. Max, we know absolutely nothing about him. I mean nothing beyond that he works security, and nobody ever remembers him. Even the police. He could do anything and get away with it. Look how people are making a wide berth around him and they go quiet. It's flaky."

"I don't understand it, but it's an incredible skill to have. Min, you don't really suspect him, do you?"

"Of course not. He's a sweet man, and so kind, and he helped at Lydstock. Remember him stage-diving?"

"How could I forget? He was the best."

"I bet he's got lots to tell us. Come on." Min grabbed my shirt and practically dragged me over to the man-mountain who turned as we approached, as if he sensed us, his smile widening.

Anxious ran ahead and Moose, clearly showing off, did the splits so he was down on the little chap's level, then bent forward at the waist until his large belly scraped the floor.

"Wow!" gasped Min.

"Wow indeed."

Moose reversed his impressive feat of gymnastics, then clicked his boots together and grinned. "Hey, guys. Great to see you."

"You too," I said. "I never knew you could do the splits."

"I can do plenty of things you don't know about," he guffawed.

I had no idea what he meant and wasn't about to ask. "Can you take a break so we can chat, or are you busy?"

"I'm busy, but nobody will notice if I take an early break," he laughed, and I was sure that was true.

Moose led us around the side of the dodgems platform, then squeezed between two trucks before taking a right and stopping at a large portacabin. He opened the door and peered inside then turned and said, "Coast's clear," and entered.

We followed Anxious inside what was clearly a staff room for the security with high-vis jackets hung on hooks and a small kitchen area stocked high with junk food, a kettle, numerous varieties of tea and coffee, and a battered old fridge.

"Our company likes to ensure we stay hydrated," said Moose, nodding at the stack of water bottles in the corner, "although, and this is just between us, half the guys and gals prefer the beer to water, even when on duty."

"Is that allowed?" asked Min.

"No, but as long as they pace themselves our boss turns a blind eye. It's not easy always being on the road, going from place to place, and if it means he keeps his staff then he's fine with it. I don't drink much myself, and never on duty." Moose slumped into a blue plastic chair and indicated we should take a seat. Anxious didn't need asking twice, so hopped up next to Moose then spun a few times before settling with a happy groan and closing his eyes.

We sat on the faded and scratched plastic chairs, facing Moose. He placed his hands in his lap and folded them over each other, looking like a Buddha, but in black rather than a loincloth. He smiled benevolently, as if awaiting our confessions.

"Have you found anything out?" asked Min, leaning forward, eager to hear his news.

"There's been plenty of talk, but not much in the way of anything that furthers the investigation. Mostly it's been the staff complaining about being accused. They don't like the police, as over the years they've had so many run-ins."

"So nobody's said anything that can help? No insights into why Leanne might have been killed?"

"I'm afraid not." Moose frowned, but it was short-lived as he couldn't keep his positive attitude at bay for long. "But there's definitely something going on."

"How do you mean?" I asked, keen to hear this enigmatic man's thoughts.

"It's hard to explain, but there's a change in atmosphere. I don't just mean because of the killing and everyone being perturbed. There's a shift in the general atmosphere. As though secrets are being kept."

"About the killing?"

"Now that's where it gets interesting. I don't think it's just about Leanne. Lash has been more grumpy than usual, but it's to hide his feelings for Leanne, I'm sure."

"I knew it!" shouted Min. "Moose, Leanne's niece showed up last night and she told us all about her and Lash."

"What's this?" he asked, shifting his bulk and making the chair creak ominously.

We explained what happened the previous evening and that morning and how Joy insisted Lash knew Leanne along with many other fairground staff, but that it was a once-a-year thing and went no further as far as she knew. Moose listened with interest, then closed his eyes and leaned back once we'd finished.

We waited, and finally his eyes opened and his round cheeks became like two balls as he grinned. "So we have a suspect. At least it's a start."

"But you don't think it was Lash, do you? And neither do we," I said.

"No. Lash might be dour and money-obsessed, but he's not the killing type. He's got a reputation as a fighter, and is good. I've seen him deal with troublemakers and he's the opposite of how he acts usually. He gets calm, and keeps his cool, and handles the problem without any overt violence. He's had too many encounters with the authorities over the years to risk getting into trouble. I can't see him doing it."

"Maybe you're right. We should still talk to him. And Chuck again. They might have some new ideas now they've had a chance to think about it."

"I spoke to both earlier, and most other staff," said Moose with a frown. "Lash was just keen to open. He was right about one thing, and that was that the killing would bring in record numbers. He hiked up the price for the haunted house and people are paying without a quibble."

"We just came from there," said Min with a tut. "It's awful to be cashing in on poor Leanne's death like that."

"It's certainly been a way to boost the income generated," sighed Moose.

"But we still don't think it was Lash?" I asked. "He's profiting from the death, so it's worked out well for him."

"Apart from the fact she was a friend," Moose reminded me.

"Yes, but how much did he value Leanne over money?" I wondered.

We spoke a little more, and invited him to dinner that evening, then we exited the portacabin and he returned to work while we decided to wander around and chat with a few people.

We found Lash at the side of a kiosk by a horrendous looking ride that seemingly just spun people around then reversed direction and slammed them into the side of the steel cage they were strapped into. I honestly couldn't imagine it being fun, and judging by the groans and green faces of those exiting, I was right. Min's eyes lit up, however, and I could tell she wanted to try it.

"Let's have a word with Lash, then you can go on if you fancy it? You wanted to try out all the rides."

"It wouldn't feel right after what's happened. Disrespectful."

"Min, you're still allowed to have fun. Leanne's murder was dreadful, but it wasn't our fault and we're doing what we can. Maybe you should go on? I'll stand here and wave as you puke your way around," I teased.

"Silly," she giggled. "I've got a stomach of steel. I never get sick from rides."

"I know, and it still amazes me. Who's Lash talking to?"

We hung back and watched as he spoke with a man in dirty jeans and a torn brown vest. Both were staying out of sight near the rear of the kiosk and kept glancing around, keeping close to one another and talking quietly. There was clearly an issue as both men had their fists clenched, their body language making it clear neither was happy.

The man shook his head of straggly dark hair, poked his finger into Lash's chest, snapped something at him, then stormed off, leaving Lash shaking his head and rubbing at his face.

"He looks stressed," whispered Min.

"He sure does. Come on, let's talk to him now. See what he has to say for himself."

We hurried over with Anxious by our side, then he barked a greeting and sat in front of Lash expectantly. The funfair owner glanced down, clearly distracted by his conversation, and muttered something before his features softened and he smiled then ruffled Anxious' fur, which seemed to placate my best buddy, as he wandered around to the back of the kiosk, sniffing as he trailed a scent us humans would never experience.

"It's you," grumbled Lash, glancing after the man who'd left.

"It is. How are you doing?" I asked.

"Been better. Been worse." He glared at us, but said nothing more.

"We met Joy, Leanne's niece. She's staying at the campsite and was shocked to hear the news. Nobody had told her. She was in bed, but we woke her and had to explain."

Lash's features softened as he put his hand to his heart. "That poor girl. She's a sweet kid and I bet she's distraught."

"Why didn't you mention yesterday that you knew Leanne and the family?" asked Min.

"Because I don't know you, and what business is it of yours?" he snapped. "I told the police all I knew, and that Leanne was a lovely woman who I liked a lot. I knew her mum, brother, and niece, but that doesn't mean I'd think to explain things to two strangers who seem way too interested in the murder."

"We just want to help get justice," said Min.

"Aye, well, that's great and all, but in case you haven't noticed, I've got other things on my mind. Leanne will be missed, and I want to find the killer the same as everyone else, but I'm also a realist."

"And that's why you opened the haunted house and are making serious money," I said, knowing it sounded accusatory.

"Don't you even consider judging me!" he growled. "This is my life, my business. All I have. What I've worked for since a lad. I will not let her terrible death ruin me. You don't know me, so don't dare judge. Something like this could be the end of it. The fair is a dying tradition, and I will not be one of the countless others that go bankrupt as everyone prefers video games and staring at their phone to actually being out and enjoying themselves."

"I'm sorry. That came out wrong," I said. "And of course you're right. But you have to admit it's not exactly honouring her memory."

"I'm doing what I have to so this place remains a proper business. I have staff to pay, mouths to feed, people to look after. Half my team are broken in one way or another, and it's my responsibility to protect them. Understand? This isn't your average place of work, and the people are struggling to cope with life, so give me a break."

"We know you work hard," soothed Min, "and we know it's a hard life, but we also know that someone killed Leanne in the haunted house and most likely it was someone she knew."

"That's bleedin' obvious, isn't it? Course she knew them. It was too nasty to be anything but premeditated, so they were after her for some reason. Look, you two, it's admirable you wanna help, but you're focusing on the wrong guy."

"What about that man you were just talking to? Who was he?" I asked.

"He works the stalls. Usually the tin can range. He's annoyed that he's got to work a longer shift, so was giving me grief about it. No big deal."

"Has he been with you long?" I asked, trying not to sound nosy and knowing I'd failed.

"Years. He's trouble, but he's family. You get me? We're all one big, happy, utterly dysfunctional family. I look after them. Am I making myself clear here? We're a family." Lash bristled as he looked me in the eye, daring me to question him.

"I understand totally. It's a lot of responsibility on your shoulders and you're doing what you can to keep things going. Sorry if we came across as rude or like we didn't understand. We do. If there's anything we can do to help, please ask. We're going to enjoy the rides, at least Min is, and I'm going to have fun on the dodgems, but please understand we only want to help."

Lash's shoulders relaxed and he gave us a half-smile, then turned to leave. "Fine."

"Oh, one more thing," I said casually. He turned back to me, clearly keen to be on his way. "How well do you know Gaz?"

Lash's eyebrows crawled up his head as he asked, "Why do you want to involve him?"

"Just asking. What can you tell us?"

"You'll want to speak to Gaz if you want to know about the lad. He's the kid dressed like a zombie. He's due on at the haunted house in an hour but is doing the rounds at the moment, getting his picture taken with the kids, jumping out at them on the rides, and just milling about and trying to shirk his work. Go easy on him though. He's a kid with a troubled past and kind of sullen and prone to clamming up, so don't expect many answers from him." With a nod, Lash hurried off. I noted his limp, so he really did have a bad hip.

"Let's go find us a zombie," I said, grinning at Min.

"Good idea. I think Lash is on the level. What about

you?"

"I think you're right. He's a grump, but he loves his funfair and family. He's doing what he can to keep his head above water. He's right about the decline of these places. Remember when we were young and there was always a fair coming to town? And go back another generation and they were the highlight of the year. There were always travelling fairs and the circus came to town a few times a year too. Now they've nearly all gone. It must be difficult to make a living. He really does care about his staff."

"He does. I'm not saying I agree with him cashing in on Leanne's death, but I do get it. Hey, where's Anxious got to?"

Right on cue, Anxious barked from behind the kiosk then came tearing towards us and skidded to a halt at our feet, barking insistently and already spinning around. We knew the sound of his warning bark, so followed as he raced off around the back past an oversized trailer for one of the rides, so with a worried look at each other, we gave chase.

We ran from the light of the funfair to a murky shadow world behind the scenes. Anxious ducked under towing bars and leapt random piles of metal, skirted a tire, then vanished.

"He's really worried about something," panted Min as she leapfrogged a barrel and raced ahead.

"Be careful! Wait for me!" I shouted as she grabbed a pole and used it to propel herself to the right, further into the gloom of the densely packed vehicles and trailers. I had to slow as my size meant I was going to crack my head on something, so ducked under a protruding lever high on an oversized trailer then followed.

Min's scream made my heart freeze and the sounds of the fair receded; all I could hear was her cry of fear. I turned right and found myself almost wedged between two trailers, the high sides of the vehicles used to transport the rides making it almost like night. But one of the floodlights managed to shine down on the narrow gap and Min and Anxious cast long shadows away from me. Both were stock still as I approached cautiously.

"Are you okay?"

"Fine. I got the fright of my life though."

"What is it?"

Min turned to me, her face ashen, dark shadows making her look like she'd applied ghoulish makeup, then she flattened herself to the trailer so I could see.

I stared at the corpse in horror. His head was caved in and blood had pooled in a dark stain on the rough ground. He wore ragged clothes splattered in blood, fake or real it was impossible to tell. Heavy makeup on his face and the fact he was carrying what I hoped was a fake arm shining under the glare of the light made it obvious who this was.

"I guess we found our zombie."

Chapter 12

"He's carrying someone's arm. There must be another body," whispered Min, her eyes two pinpoints of sharp light.

"It's fake. At least I think it is." I bent and inspected the blood-covered limb clutched by the wrist of the deceased zombie. The stump was ragged and bloody, too, but it was obviously made of rubber, although very realistic.

"Don't touch it!" warned Min, her voice so low I almost missed it.

"Don't worry, I won't. Why is he still holding it though?"

Min bent beside me, her face turned away, then slowly she studied the arm before raising her eyes to take in the terrible mess of the young man's head. "It is weird he's still holding it. Surely he would have dropped it when he was attacked?"

"Look at the hand. Not his, the rubber one. It's got fresh blood on it. I'm guessing he used it to try to defend himself. He most likely swung it and caught the killer."

"Or it's his own and the killer used it to beat Gaz. That was his name, wasn't it?"

"Yes. What was he doing hiding away back here in the shadows?" I studied the poor man, but my eyes kept being drawn to his head and the pool of congealed blood. Flies were already buzzing, drawn to the protein-rich liquid.

"Maybe he wanted some quiet time."

"Maybe." I forced myself to look away from his head, the sight nightmarish, and instead focused on the rest of him. His shirt was soaked with blood, especially around his shoulders, with plenty of fake blood across his ripped white shirt, purposely made to be tattered and grubby. His jeans were frayed and full of holes, with black Doc Martens with chunky red laces finishing off the look. It was an impressive outfit, with fake stitches at his wrists like Frankenstein's monster, the same at his throat where multiple silver necklaces and pendants gave him a real punk vibe, and I assumed were what he wore even when not in costume.

"What's that?" Something glinted beside him and we scooted over to discover a lighter.

"Maybe he was a smoker. Come back here to have a quick ciggie?"

"See if you can find anything," I suggested, already scanning the ground. We stood, and let our eyes roam while Anxious remained still, seemingly understanding the seriousness of the situation and that we shouldn't disturb things.

"There!" Min shifted carefully to the side, back to the trailer, and I followed. We both bent by the wheel and noted an open pack of rolling tobacco, the usual health warning on display.

Tobacco had spilled out, revealing a pack of rolling papers and a tube containing filters.

"He must have been about to roll up when he got disturbed and dropped the packet," I said.

"Then retrieved the arm and tried to fight?" asked Min dubiously.

"Maybe. But that would mean the first blow wasn't so serious that he couldn't try to fight them off. What could he have been hit with?"

"Anything hard, but whoever did it must have been quite strong to cause so much damage." Min glanced back at Gaz and shuddered before turning away.

"It's best not to look. Come on, we need to call the police, and I want to get into the light. It's so dark and oppressive here." I took Min's hand and carefully we returned to the still-stationary Anxious who wagged sadly at us.

"Are you alright?" Min asked as she squatted and stroked his head.

Anxious lifted his nose and sniffed then whined, clearly upset by the death. When Min moved her hand away he stood, shook himself out, then walked away. We followed, and it was with great relief that we emerged into the sunshine. The noise of the funfair returned as though the sound had been muted while we were deep in its underbelly.

It felt strange to see everyone going about their business, happy and laughing, faces flushed or green after the rides. Children ate candy floss and hotdogs, oblivious to the terrible murder that had just been committed.

"It's very surreal," noted Min. "It always is. It's the same with Leanne. I just couldn't reconcile what I was seeing with the reality. That it really happened."

"It's because it's so out of the norm. You see people breathing, not just gone. It's hard to adjust. To accept they're genuinely dead."

"But you must be able to handle it easier now. You've seen so much of it."

"Not really. It gets easier to deal with what I'm seeing, but it always feels surreal, like they're no more real than that arm Gaz was holding. What do you think about Lash being around the corner from where this happened? And that man he was with?"

"It's either a mighty coincidence or one of them did it. What were they arguing about? I bet it wasn't just about long shifts."

"He won't tell us. He'll say it's none of our business. But we'll have to tell the police. I won't hide that from the Susans."

"No way. They need to know," agreed Min. "We should call. Should we phone them or the regular police?"

"I think we should phone Susie. She'll know what to do and can arrange things. I'll call now." Knowing it had to be done, but feeling reluctant, I pulled out my phone and made the call. Susie took it in her usual lighthearted way, but asked me to ensure nobody disturbed the scene until an officer arrived. She said she'd get someone already on site to come over, and to wait until they arrived then stay close so she and Sue could speak to us in person.

Reluctantly, we moved back into the strange other world behind the scenes of the fair, but waited far enough away from the body so we didn't have to look at Gaz but could see anyone coming our way. People passed by without a second glance, as why would anyone want to come back here when the fun was out in the light where it was warm and cheery?

Min shivered and moved closer to me. Anxious whined but sat bravely, eyes roaming for suspects, and behaving impeccably. He let out a small bark and I noted Chuck heading towards us, glancing over his shoulder before putting his head down and increasing his speed as though he could blend with the crowd despite wearing his terrifying clown costume.

"Here comes Chuck," I told Min, indicating him with a nod.

"He's heading straight for us. Why is he coming here?"

"We're about to find out. First Leanne, and now Gaz, and he's on the scene for both murders."

"Why would he return if it was him?"

"Maybe he left something incriminating behind?"

"You don't think he did it, do you?"

"No," I admitted. "But I'm still going to ask."

Chuck ducked behind the trailer then pulled up short, eyes widening as he noticed us. Anxious growled, then looked to me for guidance, but I wanted to see what he thought so left him to make his own decision. Chuck fidgeted, glanced behind him as Anxious approached then sniffed his legs before trotting back to us and sitting, tail wagging. Chuck was in the clear as far as he was concerned, but I still wanted to have a few words.

"Um, what are you guys up to?" asked Chuck after a peculiar and long silence.

"That's what we'd like to ask you," I said. "Shouldn't you be working? I thought you were in the haunted house. Which, I have to say, seems very disrespectful."

"Terrible," agreed Min with a pout.

"Hey, don't blame me," he said, hands raised in a placatory gesture. "I didn't want to work today, but Lash insisted. We had a massive row when he returned from the shops to get treats for everyone. He said he'd lost a fortune yesterday and had to do something to boost the earnings or we'd be out of business soon enough. He really pushed for us to open, and if I want to keep my job I do what I'm told." Chuck tugged at the garish plastic yellow flower at his lapel while he swung his fake axe with the other hand, clearly stressed.

"Why are you looking so worried?" asked Min. "You look guilty."

"Er, I'm not meant to be here. My shift isn't over for hours, but I needed a smoke. Me and Gaz always meet at this time and I'm late. He gets annoyed if I don't arrive on time, and if Lash finds out we'll both be in trouble. It's hard to hide when you're dressed as a killer clown, and everyone keeps stopping me and asking for selfies. It's gross. They're enjoying the drama, and it's madness in the haunted house. It's never been so busy. Look, I gotta go. Gaz will be annoyed."

Chuck went to leave, but I put a hand to his

shoulder gently and said, "We have to tell you something first. I'm sorry, but Gaz is dead."

"Shut up!" he laughed, but his smile faded when we didn't join in. "For real?"

"Yes, for real. Someone murdered him. There's no doubt. It has to be the same person. Was it you, Chuck? Did you kill him?"

"What!? No way! He's my best mate. Let me see." With a determined grunt, Chuck brushed past us.

"Don't get too close," I shouted, then we hurried after him before he disturbed the scene and made a terrible situation even worse.

We didn't have to go far before we caught up with him at the end of the trailer where he was bent over and sobbing. When Min put her hand to his arm he stood and wiped his face, smearing the already smudged makeup and making his face truly frightening. I would not want to meet him in a dark alley, and I shuddered as I realised where we were and that whatever he did, it might be a ploy to hide his own guilt.

"We're so sorry about this," soothed Min. "Were you very close?"

"He was my best buddy. We had such a laugh together and now he's dead. It doesn't make any sense. Who would do this? And look at him! His head's caved in." Chuck sniffed and wiped his nose with his sleeve, but couldn't avert his gaze.

"Maybe we should go?" I suggested. "You don't need to see him like this. Have a smoke to calm your nerves. That's what you said you were coming here for, right?"

"Yeah, of course. We always had a few sneaky ciggies through the day. It's long hours and we don't get enough breaks, so we pull unofficial ones when we can. Everyone does it." Chuck patted his pockets looking for his tobacco, but frowned.

"Problem?"

"Can't find my baccy. I must have left it with my

gear at the haunted house. Weird."

"Very. How could you forget it?"

"I'm all over the place today. It hit hard, you know? Losing Leanne like that. She was a kind woman and everyone thought a lot of her."

"And she knew Gaz?"

"Eh? Um, yeah, a little," he said, his tone cautious.

"Or quite well?" suggested Min. "Chuck, did they know each other properly, or just to say hello to? It's important. There has a to be a link between them."

"He knew her like I did. Just to say hi to, have a bit of banter, but they weren't proper friends or anything. How could they be? We come here once, maybe twice a year, and always saw her, but she was older than us and we've both only been with the fair a few years compared to most of the old-timers."

"That makes sense," said Min, glancing at me to get my opinion.

"Is there anything you can think of that links them?" I asked. "Anything at all?"

"Not that I can think of. Like I said, we knew her a little as she was a face at the fair. She loved it so much, and apparently her mum was the same. Lash knew them both well, the whole family, actually, as he was always chasing after her. But nothing sinister," he added hurriedly. "He was always respectful to Leanne. Lash is a tough guy, but he was like a puppy when she was around."

"So why would anyone kill her and Gaz? Was he into anything that might get him into trouble?" I wondered.

"Gaz? No way. He was squeaky clean. Okay, maybe not totally straight, but he was a decent guy and never got into bother. He did his work, tried to have a good time, and that was it. Now he's gone." Chuck looked at the corpse of his friend again and shook his head sadly.

"Let's move away. The police will be here soon. I bet they'll close the fair again, and I doubt Lash will be allowed to re-open today."

"Good. Someone needs to figure out why this happened."

We led Chuck back to the edge of the trailer and he sat on the ground with his legs crossed and his head bowed, lost in his own thoughts as we waited in silence.

A police officer arrived soon after and then another two, and they secured the area while we explained the situation. Nobody touched the body after the officer checked he was definitely dead, but then the on-site paramedics arrived and performed proper checks then declared him dead. We were asked to move away while the officers performed a preliminary search, but nothing too intense as that was for the detectives to do.

Chuck had removed his wig and red nose, and if anything it made him appear more terrifying with his smeared makeup and the fake stitches and cuts on his face, then a clean head of hair and a pale patch on his nose. His axe lay in his lap where he now sat leaning against the back of a truck, head down.

"What should we do?" asked Min.

"I don't know what we can do to help him. He needs to grieve. It's strange he forgot his tobacco, though, if that's why he came."

"You think he might be guilty of it?"

"No, but I'm not sure he's telling the truth about being a smoker. No way would he forget his stuff if he was."

"Why else would he be coming here then? Why lie about it?"

"I don't know if he is lying, but it's odd, for sure." I couldn't quite understand why this didn't ring true, but something was bugging me. Was he even a smoker? It wasn't very common nowadays, especially with the younger generation.

"There they are!" declared Susie as she beamed at us, Sue by her side. Today, her partner sported a gold synthetic jumpsuit with matching eye makeup and blusher with glitter at her cheeks, making her look like she'd just come from an eighties roller disco.

"Right in the thick of things as usual," laughed Sue as she high-fived her drab partner.

"Chuck's taking this very hard," I told them, astonished by their behaviour even though I shouldn't have been now. "They were good friends."

"Gosh, and here we are smiling," said Sue, trying to tame her expression and failing. "We're sorry for your loss."

"Thanks," mumbled Chuck. "He was a great guy and didn't deserve this."

"Of course he didn't. Nobody does. Now, you wait here while we take a look, then we'll ask you a few questions," said Susie, playing the compassionate elder woman perfectly even though there was a sparkle in her eye and Sue kept nudging her in the side like she was dying to share a joke. I couldn't figure these two out at all.

Sue skipped off ahead like she couldn't wait to get to the corpse, while Susie pulled her cardigan tight around her then followed, a spring in her step too.

"That pair are weird," said Chuck, using the trailer for support as he stood. "What's with them?"

"I honestly don't know," I admitted. "They're good at their job, but are definitely not your usual detectives."

"They never seem to be anything but happy," said Min. "You'd expect them to be stressed and looking tired after yesterday, but they're so upbeat."

"It's not normal," grumbled Chuck. "Nobody's that happy."

Several minutes later, the two Susans returned, and this time their expressions were much more sombre.

"A terrible business," said Susie.

"Awful," agreed Sue. "Can we have a word with you all? Max and Min, you discovered the body didn't you?"

We explained what'd happened, and what we saw, which was nothing beyond Gaz and before that Lash talking with the mystery man, which caused the detectives to exchange a look, but they kept any opinions to themselves. It seemed like they didn't want to say much in front of Chuck. Once he'd told them why he was here, they said he could leave, but that he was to keep quiet about this until they'd gone over the scene properly. He hurried off, keen to put some distance between him and his deceased friend, leaving us with the detectives.

"Now," said Sue, rubbing her hands together, "what do we think happened here?"

"How'd you mean?" I asked.

"Come on, Max," said Sue, "you must have an opinion. You, too, Min. What are we thinking? Chuck possibly? He's now been at both crime scenes."

"He's acting oddly, but I don't think it was him. I'm guessing whoever did this got hurt by Gaz. There was blood on the fake arm and I'm thinking maybe he used it to defend himself."

"Well spotted," said Susie with a chuckle. She turned to Sue and said, "He really is very good, isn't he?"

"A keen eye," she agreed. "What else?"

"He was coming for a smoke but got disturbed. Chuck said they met up at this time to have a sneaky break, and he must have been expecting him but someone else got here first."

"Most likely someone who knew they both took an unofficial break," said Min.

"Yes, that's probably it," agreed Susie. "Whoever did this must have known he would be here."

"Or they followed him," corrected Sue.

"Great call!" beamed Susie. She turned to us and said, "We've got a lot to go over, so we'll speak later, but keep working the case and keep talking to people. Someone must know something."

"If it's all the same with you, we're going to pop back to the shops, pick up a few things, then try to relax at the campsite. It's been hectic since yesterday and we need some down time."

"Great idea. You go and enjoy yourselves, but don't forget about us."

With a smile from the DSs, they left us alone and we hurried into the light and noise, keen to escape the stench of death.

Chapter 13

Anxious couldn't get away from the funfair quick enough. The volume of visitors was astonishing, even if it was turning into a very pleasant afternoon, at least as far as the weather went. He rushed ahead, turning regularly to check on us, and I didn't have the heart to put the little guy on the lead as it would make it harder for him to dodge legs.

We needed to pick a few things up for dinner and I had to buy new cloths, so we regrouped on the grass for a while just watching the streams of people descending on the fair. Some to have fun, but plenty out of morbid curiosity, with the majority heading straight for the haunted house.

"They'll be closed down soon," I told Min.

"And so they should be. I know they need to make money, but it's horrid seeing Leanne's death turned into a money-maker."

"Let's go to that hardware shop we saw earlier," I suggested, knowing Min loved those kinds of places.

"Ooh, great," she beamed. "Did you see all the plastic containers and buckets they had outside? And they had so many brooms and galvanised things. I do love a bit of galvanising."

"Stop it, you're practically drooling," I teased. "Why do you love these shops so much?"

"Because they have a little of everything. You never know what you'll find. And it makes me feel like I'm stepping back in time. Shops used to always be like that. Proper family businesses, not corporate copies of each other. They're all different and they're such fun."

We strolled down the high street, enjoying the peace, the receding noise of the funfair making life feel dreamlike, as though nothing bad could possibly have happened on such a sunny afternoon. When we arrived at the shop we grinned at each other, and even Anxious was keen to explore, so investigated the plastic boxes, the buckets, the bins full of other smaller bins, and when he spied the pile of mops he became quite animated. Maybe he thought they were mini dogs because he sure gave them a good sniff.

Inside was cool and absolutely rammed with just about everything you could think of that wasn't food. We moved slowly, careful of the racks and shelves stocked high, and took our time perusing the numerous aisles. I often wondered how anyone actually found what they were looking for in such places, but judging by the bemused expressions of the customers, and the confused looks on their faces as they clutched random items, I laughed as I realised they were the same as us and most likely didn't even know what they wanted until they spied some esoteric item high on a shelf and decided they absolutely needed it.

"Isn't it awesome here?" cooed Min, fawning over a stack of plastic boxes.

"They sure do have all sorts. Look, they even have balls for horses."

"Balls!"

"They do. Over there." I pointed to the large red balls with the sign above explaining what they were.

"No, I meant, oh, wow, horse balls." Min smiled as she fondled a dustpan and brush, then laughed.

"Are you being cheeky?" I teased, unable to resist picking up a small stackable collection of containers I had absolutely no use for but was tempted to buy even though I had no explanation as to why.

"As if. Hey, think we should get two of these?" Min picked up what looked like half an umbrella and opened it out.

"You can't do that!" I took a step back and searched the aisle for fear of falling objects.

"You aren't superstitious. Don't be silly. It's an umbrella that slips onto your head. See?"

Min placed the little cap on her head and giggled as she twirled, making Anxious excited so he ran around her, tail wagging.

"You don't open umbrellas indoors. It's nothing to do with being superstitious, it's just what you don't do. Imagine if we walked around Leanne's campsite wearing those things. We'd be a laughingstock."

"Excuse me, dear?"

I turned to find an elderly lady dressed in tweed with a thick head of silver hair smiling up at me. She was wiry and barely over five feet, but her ruddy complexion and muscular forearms peeking from beneath her shirt rolled up to mid-forearm signified she was a hard worker and most likely a local farmer.

"Yes, what can I do for you?" I asked. "Sorry for the open umbrella. I warned her."

"It's very bad luck, dearie," she admonished, wagging a finger at Min but smiling.

"Sorry. I was just having fun." Min folded up the umbrella and replaced it on the shelf while Anxious came over to meet our new friend.

"He's adorable. Hello there. Would you like a biscuit?"

Anxious immediately sat and locked his eyes on the dirty pocket the woman was already fishing around in.

"You can take that as a yes," I laughed.

"I always carry a few. I have three Border Collies

and never go anywhere without them. They're waiting by the Land Rover as they get too excited in shops, but I needed to pick up a few bits and pieces." She handed the treat to Anxious who took it gently and wagged in thanks then settled down to enjoy his snack.

"They're great dogs. Anxious here is usually well-behaved, but he does excite easily."

"Anxious? Oh, the poor dear. What happened?"

"Nothing. It's his name, not his emotional state. Sometimes I wish we'd called him something different as I've had to explain so many times."

"Me too. Hi." Min smiled at the lady and shook her hand when it was offered. I did the same and made introductions. Pam explained that she lived not far from Leanne's and had seen us coming and going, and then she went quiet and her eyes lowered as she fidgeted, clearly wanting to say something.

"Is there a problem?" I asked.

"It's rather delicate, actually. Um, I was so sad to hear what happened to poor Leanne, and such a shock to everyone."

"Did you know her?" I asked.

"A little. Not a lot, as who has the time for visits? But we chatted now and then and she gave me some of her crop last year. That's, er, what I wanted to ask. Not from you, mind you, but if you could ask Joy. I hear she's up at the campsite now and is such a great girl."

"I'm not following," I admitted, wondering why Pam was acting so nervous about things.

"It's, er, well, I wondered if you'd ask Joy if she would make sure to save me some, er, wheat."

"Wheat?" asked Min with a frown at Pam and a raised eyebrow for me.

"Yes. For making bread. Leanne always did a small field of it. Nothing much, just a hobby really, and last year she let me have some. It was the best, er, bread I ever had.

Really did the job. Would you remind Joy to save some for me as I suppose she'll take over things now. She will, won't she? I wouldn't want strangers up there. She's practically a neighbour."

"We can ask her," said Min kindly, "but she hasn't mentioned any wheat."

"Thank you, dearie, that's all I ask," beamed Pam, wiping at her forehead and looking relieved. "Well, must be off. Things to do, animals to tend. I may be old, but farmers' wives don't retire, as their husbands never do," she tittered, suddenly coy, a hand to her mouth.

"Nice to meet you, Pam," I said.

"Yes, and we'll be sure to ask Joy about the wheat," said Min.

"Lovely. That's great!" with a spring in her step, Pam hurried off, leaving us confused.

"What was that all about?" whispered Min, poking her head around the aisle to ensure Pam was out of earshot.

"No idea. Joy hasn't mentioned wheat, and why was Pam so nervous about mentioning it?"

"It was weird. Maybe we should ask Joy."

"We will. You don't think…"

"What?"

"Nothing. I was just being silly."

"Come on, spit it out." Min tugged at my arm and smiled.

"Maybe it was code for something. Maybe she doesn't mean wheat."

"Then what could she mean?"

"I have no idea. Come on, let's get what we need then go ask Joy. We should get back anyway. I want to get dinner on and I need to stop thinking about murders for a while."

"Me too. It's been a very odd and stressful day and it will be great to relax."

We found the cloths and paid, then after hurriedly

buying the rest of what we needed for dinner returned to Vee. Min said she fancied driving so took us back up the hill slowly, navigated the lanes like a pro, and soon we arrived at the campsite. After parking at our pitch, we wandered over to the house and found Joy outside in the front garden.

"Are you both okay? I heard what happened. It's truly awful. What is happening around here?" Joy placed her trowel on the garden wall and sighed as she picked at her dirty nails.

"It was terrible," said Min. "The poor man was in an awful state. We don't know who did it, but it can't be a coincidence."

"It can't, can it?" agreed Joy as she rubbed her hands on her jeans then took a sip from a water bottle. "Did you find anything out? Does anyone know anything? I got a call from the detectives, both of them on the line, and it was rather confusing."

"How so?" I asked.

"They said they were calling to tell me about the murder today, but also wanted to know if Leanne had any links to this Gaz."

"And did she?"

"Not that I know of. But they seemed to think she did for some reason. They were quite insistent."

"That doesn't sound like them," noted Min. "And why were they calling you to tell you about the murder?"

"I think they're convinced the deaths were related and they warned me to be on my guard. They didn't say it outright, but I got the feeling they think I might be next." Joy's eyes drifted from us to the gate and lane, then she sighed and a staccato laugh escaped her pursed lips. "I can't think why anyone would want to hurt me, but then I can't think why anyone would kill my aunty or that young lad either."

"He was your age, wasn't he?" I asked.

"About the same, yes. I told the detectives that I only knew him to say hello to at the funfair the same as Leanne did, at least as far as I know."

"You should take them seriously and be careful," said Min. "Don't talk to strangers."

Joy laughed as she said, "That's a bit difficult when you run a campsite. Everyone who comes here is a stranger. What am I supposed to do? I don't want to turn people away if they want to stay, but I'm not even sure if I'm allowed to let them. I need to look into things and see about insurance and all that, but obviously I can't do any of that until I even know if Aunty left things to me or not. Maybe she left everything to a local dog rescue centre. I doubt it, but you never know."

"True, but from what she said about you and what you've told us, you're probably right and the place is yours. As to insurance, I have no idea. It can't hurt to let people stay, though, I assume, but maybe it is best to close until this is solved."

"No!" Joy put her hands on her hips and added, "That's not what Aunty would have wanted. She wouldn't want me to let whoever did this think they'd won."

"If the campsite had anything to do with it," I said. "Oh, by the way, what do you know about wheat?"

"Wheat?" Joy frowned, but she looked away and towards the side of the house where a high hedge hid the fields.

"We met a woman called Pam in the hardware shop and she was acting strangely," explained Min. "She recognised us from coming up and down the lane and asked us to mention it to you. Apparently, she had some wheat from Leanne last year and was promised the same this year, too, and wanted us to ask you if it was still okay."

"Um, I guess." Joy shrugged, and again glanced towards the fields.

"What is it?" asked Min, picking up on her strange behaviour.

"Nothing, but I better get on. The weeds seem to have gone crazy and I'm determined to make the garden the best it's ever looked. Aunty had green fingers and could get anything to grow, but I'm not as gifted. I'm going to make sure the garden stays how she wanted it, so have to keep it clear of weeds."

Min and I exchanged a look, then I said in a gentle tone, "Joy, we know you're hiding something from us. What is it? You want the killer found, don't you?"

"Of course I do, but this has nothing to do with that."

"You're being very evasive and cryptic," said Min patiently. "We want to help. If there's something wrong, you can tell us. What are you hiding?"

"I told you, it's nothing to do with her murder. It's, er. No, it's nothing." Joy shook her head and picked up her trowel, clearly trying to get us to leave.

"What if it is to do with her murder? What if it's a link to what's been happening? You should tell us."

"Fine, but I guess I better show you, not tell you. I only found out about it today, and it's a shock. I guess Leanne was struggling or wanted a way to earn extra money, so she, er… Come on, let me show you. But you have to promise not to tell. I don't want anyone thinking badly of her."

"We can't promise anything," I said. "We don't know what you're talking about. But unless it could help catch her killer, we won't say anything to anyone."

"I guess that will have to do then. Follow me." Joy put her trowel back down, came through the gate, and turned left with us trailing behind, confused and rather wary of what we were about to be shown.

After glancing back, Joy opened a small gate in the hedgerow and ducked beneath the dense hawthorn above. Anxious followed along merrily, excited by an adventure. We trailed after him, senses heightened, nervous about what we were letting ourselves in for, but I could tell by the sparkle in Min's eyes that she was as excited as me.

"Make sure you close the gate," called Joy as she

crept through the very thick hedge. It must have been at least five plants deep, the trunks and branches of the hawthorn interwoven to make an almost impenetrable fence.

I clicked it shut and ducked low, crept through the hedge, then emerged into bright light.

"Um, it really is just wheat," I said, disappointed.

"We thought there was going to be something else."

"Like what?" asked Joy.

"I'm not sure," I admitted.

"Follow me," Joy sighed. You wouldn't know it was there if you weren't looking, but there was a slight path that Joy used, so we followed in single file, the dried stalks and heads of the wheat bursting with seed rustling as we brushed past them. Surely it should have been harvested already?

Without even realising, I suddenly noted the difference in temperature and that it was slightly shaded now. When I looked up, I was astonished to discover that we were underneath some form of canopy. It stretched out in all directions, and when I sniffed I got the unmistakable tang of something all-too-familiar at music festivals. I took notice of what was growing, and blurted, "She's growing marijuana?"

"Looks like it. It's not exactly a massive operation, but I counted at least twenty plants. She's even set up camouflage netting. I sent up a drone earlier and it's the same colour as the wheat, so from the air it looks like the rest of the field."

"I didn't think she grew crops," said Min.

"She's always grown wheat or sometimes tried other cereals. She wanted to see if she could make her own bread and stuff like that, and she cut it with a scythe. Grandma used to do the same, and every year we'd come as a family and cut it. It was great fun as we were allowed to wield these huge long scythes and swish away at the crops."

"But Leanne went from just wheat to something

extra?" I asked. "Did you know?"

"No, I did not, and I would have told her not to be so stupid. I know the laws are more relaxed about marijuana now, but she would still be in loads of trouble and might even go to prison. It's a lot for one person, and if you've got the likes of Pam asking for some, and I'm air quoting here, 'wheat', then who else was she supplying? I don't get it at all. It's crazy."

"Joy, you have to tell the police," said Min. "It might be why she was murdered."

"I can't. It'll be all over the papers. Her legacy and reputation will be ruined. I don't want people getting the wrong impression, and if this gets out she'll just be the crazy pot lady who got butchered, rather than who she was. A hard-working, beautiful, kind woman who happened to have a stealth dope farm on her property. I can't imagine what got into her."

"It doesn't sound like her at all," agreed Min. "What a risk to take. She would definitely get a criminal record and probably a prison sentence. Max, what do you think?"

Both women, and Anxious, turned to me as though I had the answers. "I'm confused. I don't think you go to jail for growing this number of plants, but I might be wrong. But if she's supplying it, that's a different matter entirely. She would definitely be in a lot of trouble. What I don't understand is why Pam knew. That's risky. Beyond risky. Why tell her how she did it even if she was selling some to her. And who else knows?"

"Maybe everyone knows," said Joy. "Maybe everyone around here is growing it."

"And maybe someone wants it for themselves so got Leanne out of the picture," gasped Min. "They might have killed her so they could come and get the crop. Is it ready?"

"I looked it up earlier, and it will probably be a few weeks yet, maybe less. Do you think this is the motive?"

"It might well be," I said cautiously, "but I can't imagine anyone would kill over a few plants. We need to speak to Pam and see what she knows. There's more to this than there seems, I'm sure of it. Joy, don't think badly of Leanne for growing a few plants. There's been a big shift in attitudes lately to marijuana, and it's even prescribed on the NHS now if they think it will help."

"I know," said Joy. "It helps some people with chronic pain and even mental health issues in some cases, but it's still illegal and she should have known better."

"It's definitely a risk, and I can't believe she went to all this trouble to hide it. It's impressive." Min moved closer to one of the plants that towered over her and sniffed. "Wow, it's so strong."

"Careful, or you'll be high as a kite," I warned.

"I'm just sniffing. Let's get out of here. It's hot and I don't like it."

I led the way back out and once we were by the house we stood there, nobody knowing quite what to say or do.

"Does your dad know?" I asked.

"No, and I wasn't going to tell him, but I think I'll have to. I don't want him getting angry about it."

"Is that likely?" asked Min.

"It's his sister, and she was a drug smuggler. He'll be livid. He's a square, and this is way over his head."

"What's way over my head?" asked Rupert as he stood clutching bags of shopping, a deep frown on his face.

Chapter 14

"Oh, didn't see you there, Dad." Joy picked up her trowel as if it could defend her against her father's ire, but judging by the deep frown and glare, it would take more than that to protect her.

"Clearly. What were you talking about?" He lowered his bags but stood his ground, eyes slowly passing along each of us.

"You should tell him," said Min, nodding and smiling.

"It's for the best," I agreed, wondering how he'd take the news. He wasn't an easy man to read, not exactly an open book, but he clearly loved his daughter and had thought the world of his sister, so it could go one of two ways.

Anxious, keen as always to keep the mood light, barked softly and planted himself in front of Rupert.

"Hey there, Anxious. What have you been up to?" asked Rupert, bending to stroke him, his eyes fixed on Joy.

Anxious explained about our little trip into the field, but Rupert just nodded then stood and glared at Joy as though the explanation wasn't quite enough. Which was understandable. Anxious often rushed his words.

"Dad, don't get cross, and it doesn't mean she wasn't a great woman, and you shouldn't think badly of her," blurted Joy, her cheeks burning as she tapped the towel on the wall.

"I don't know what you're talking about. What's wrong? Are you alright?" Rupert's hands went out as he took a step forward, but Joy stepped back to the wall then sat and hung her head. "You can tell me. It's okay." Rupert turned to me and asked, "Max, what's this about?"

"I think Joy should explain. And it's nothing to worry about. She's fine."

"That's a relief," he sighed, tugging at his lightweight waterproof then removing it. "Gosh, it's so warm now. Can't get to grips with this weather at all."

"Dad, Leanne had a dope farm. She was growing marijuana. It might be why she was murdered."

"Over a few plants?" laughed Rupert. "I doubt that very much. It's not exactly big-time gangster stuff, especially nowadays."

"You knew?" asked Joy. "You're kidding, right?" Her trowel clattered onto the top of the wall but she didn't even notice.

"What's the big deal?" asked Rupert with a shrug.

"Dad, you're about as straight as they come and always hated drugs. You don't even drink or have coffee as you say it isn't natural, and now you're cool with your sister running a dope farm?"

"Like I said, it's only a few plants. And yes, I have always warned about using drugs, and I don't like caffeine or nicotine or anything unnatural, but once Leanne explained what she was doing, and more importantly, why, then I couldn't exactly argue, could I?"

"Can you tell us?" I asked.

"Sure. I guess there's no point pretending this hasn't happened. A few years ago she told me what she was planning, and asked for my help. Whenever we came to visit, I'd do some work with her, but we never let you know, Joy, as it wasn't the easiest thing to explain."

"Did Grandma know?"

"Actually, yes. That's what gave Leanne the idea. She found it once she took over things here, and some of the locals turned up asking if she was going to continue with the harvest. She didn't know what they were talking about until they explained."

"So she was dealing drugs?" asked Min.

"No. Absolutely not. She gave to those who wanted it. My mother did the same for years, apparently, but the set-up wasn't as good and she was taking a big risk. Leanne and I set things up properly so she wouldn't get caught, and every year we'd sort out the crop, dry it, then deliver to a few neighbours. Just a few, mind you, and the rest would sit in the barn until someone wanted it. Never tried it myself, but apparently it's excellent."

"Dad, I can't believe you're acting like it's nothing. It's illegal and you could have got into a lot of trouble."

"It was worth the risk. People around here were good to your grandma, and she wanted to give something back. It helps Pam with her arthritis, says it makes it possible for her to get through the day, and for others it helps with the loneliness. They're mostly older folk, and a little pot helps them to get through the day. It's nothing different to having a glass of wine."

"It absolutely is different. Of course it is. Maybe it does help, or maybe they just like having free drugs and getting high. That's no reason to be putting yourself at risk. And now Aunty Leanne is dead."

"And that is truly awful. I can't even begin to tell you how sad it makes me, but it has nothing to do with this."

"How do you know?" I wondered. "Maybe someone doesn't like the fact she was cultivating marijuana. Maybe they wanted to put a stop to it. Who else knew? Did anyone at the funfair know?"

"Leanne mentioned something about a man called Gaz. He helped her out learning what to do. How to harvest and dry the plants. We had no idea. I certainly didn't!" he chuckled.

"And now Gaz is dead. Butchered!" wailed Joy, staggering backwards and resting against the wall, knocking the trowel off and it landed on her foot. She glanced at it, but with eyes full of tears, so I bent and picked it up then rested it on the wall.

"What? When? How did it happen?" Rupert asked me, "Were you there? You seem to always be around when something bad happens. Max, what happened?"

After I explained, Rupert was ashen, and rubbed at his red hair like he was being attacked by bugs. He bent forward and gasped for air, then straightened and smiled weakly at his daughter. "I'm so sorry. I had no idea. What is happening around here?"

"Drug deals gone wrong. That's what," screeched Joy.

"Nonsense. Whatever the reason for these killings, it isn't the crops. It's a few plants Leanne handed out to the locals. People are isolated up here and get lonely. It helps them make it through. Some of the neighbours she visited wouldn't see a soul if it wasn't for her deliveries."

"Dad, can you hear yourself? What other reason could there be? Gaz knew about it and was involved, and now he's dead. They've been murdered by rival drug dealers. Are you insane letting her get involved in something like that?"

"It wasn't a big deal," Rupert insisted. "A little medicine to help. I checked into it and if she was caught she wouldn't even go to prison as she wasn't selling anything. And we made sure not to go over twenty plants so it wasn't seen as a large operation."

"We'll check on you in the morning," I told Joy. "You two should talk, and we're in the way. Joy, take care of yourself, and don't be too hard on your dad. He was doing what he thought best, and if Leanne believed she was helping, then don't think badly of her."

"Max is right," said Min. "She was trying to help her friends. Maybe we don't all agree on if this was a smart idea, but she was trying to be a good neighbour."

"I can't believe you all. I was so worried when I found the plants and now you're all for it?"

"Not exactly, but you have to look at it from Leanne's point of view," I said. "She believed in what she did, so you have to respect that."

"I don't know if I can," Joy murmured, then flung herself at her father and he wrapped his arms around her.

We nodded our goodbyes to him as Joy sobbed into his chest, and left. The walk back to our pitch was a sombre one, as the discovery had been so unexpected. Neither Min nor I knew what to think, but if Rupert was happy with what Leanne had been up to then we were in no position to judge.

The moment we arrived, I got busy preparing dinner. We were already up against it regards time, and I didn't want to let anyone down, so slipped easily into chef mode and let go of my concerns and became immersed in cooking.

It was my meditation, my passion, my solace, and my joy. The one way I could stop thinking about anything else and be in the present, firmly locked in the moment. I peeled, chopped, sliced, diced, browned off the meat, checked on everything and seasoned as I went, always ensuring to under rather than overdo it. One of the most important lessons I'd ever learned in the kitchen was early on in my career when a wizened old chef had explained that you can always add more seasoning, but you can never take it back out.

He told me to bide my time, taste as I went, but always with the knowledge that I could add a pinch right at the end if I found anything lacking. I still cooked by that rule, and it always served me well.

Anxious slid under Vee and kept a watchful eye on proceedings for a while, but once he realised there would be no snacks until after dinner he curled up with a groan and took a nap. I could have happily joined him, as the day had been gruelling, but we had guests arriving and there was still plenty to do.

Min sorted out the small fold-out table I had stowed in the back and made it look lovely so we could all eat together, and busied herself tidying up after me so I had a clean work area, something I was fastidious about, and the flow was a thing of beauty. We were in-tune with one another and hardly said a word, just worked as a team, and it made my heart sing.

This was something I truly missed from my time in the kitchen. The flow state when everyone could anticipate everyone else's moves and act accordingly. When everything works as planned and it felt like you were being guided by a higher being. A strange thing to feel when you're arranging slices of duck or squirting sauces in fancy ways, but sometimes that was how it felt. And now I had my absolute favourite companion by my side and it was wondrous.

No stress, no worries, no thinking about the day. Just a deep, absolute focus on what had to be done right here and right now. When I finally turned the heat down on the pot and put the lid on then stepped back and sighed, I was almost euphoric. I turned to Min and smiled, and she laughed as she took my hand and squeezed.

"What was that for?" I asked, confused.

"Because it's lovely to see you like that. You were so focused, I think a bomb could have gone off and you wouldn't have even flinched. You were in the zone."

"Single-minded and obsessive, you mean? I thought you hated that stuff?"

"When it interferes with life, yes, but when you're cooking or doing chores, or whatever it might be, I think it's admirable. I'm always amazed how deep into things you get. I wish I could do the same."

"I thought you'd want me to stop obsessing?"

"Yes, and no. It's who you are, and why you're so good at the things you do, but when it goes too far it's a problem. Max, don't you see? You've cured yourself. You know when to become immersed in a project or problems, and when to ease off, take a step back, and let the rest of the world in. It's a real accomplishment." Min stood on tiptoe and planted a lovely kiss on my cheek, and I beamed with pride and happiness.

"Thank you. That means more than you will ever know."

"Oh, I know how much it means, alright, because I'm utterly awesome too."

"You really are," I agreed, grinning. "Now, how about a glass of wine and a rest? Dinner will be at least an hour, so we can finally relax. What a day. It felt like we'd never get a moment to ourselves."

"We've had hours together, silly. All morning, and plenty of time this afternoon. It hasn't exactly been stress-free, but when is it ever?"

"Never?" I offered. "I wish we could spend more time relaxing though. What do you think about this business with the plants?"

"I think it could be the reason they were killed, or it could be nothing more than what Rupert said. It seems like it's been going on for years and years. Did you know it helps with glaucoma too? And Parkinson's? That's what I heard anyway. Although, it's not exactly accepted and I get that too. It's still illegal and there are large gangs that control such things, so maybe it's why they were killed. Oh, I don't know." Min threw her arms in the air and shook her head, then smiled. "But forgot about all that for a while. Let's drink our wine, chill out, and enjoy the quiet."

"Deal."

We fell into that happy silence only two people who know each other well can enjoy without feeling the need to talk. We sipped, we sat, we watched the world go by, and it was beautiful. It might not have been a scorcher, but even with a fine drizzle and brooding clouds, it was a lovely evening. I could never tire of being out in the weather and simply being.

The entire country was my garden, and I adored it more than I expected to. The longer I lived this strange new life, the more I appreciated not only the freedom but the country I was lucky enough to be born in. I wondered if people felt the same about places that were always cold and covered in snow, or roasting hot. I supposed they did and found beauty in whatever was around them.

Teasing aromas drifted towards us from the outdoor kitchen as we enjoyed the birdsong, the rips of zips opening and closing, and the occasional burst of laughter from the few others on the campsite. Two young children, an adorable brother and sister with shockingly long straight blond hair, kicked a ball about and ran after it with squeals of laughter, whilst adults could be heard murmuring from beside their tents as they talked quietly.

It felt like the dying end of an era. Kids were back in school, so only a few youngsters were around now, and with the weather changing I knew this might be the last time I saw people in tents apart from the dedicated hikers and cyclists challenging themselves during the more inclement months. I daydreamed about walks on the beach in the winter with Anxious' ears flapping in the wind as a storm raged across the sea and waves crashed against the high walls of Aberystwyth and the lighthouse was engulfed in giant waves.

Snapshots of picturesque Cornish towns in the bleak midwinter when the tourists had gone swam past, where I walked with my buddy down steep cobbled streets and Min emerged from a sweet shop clutching a pink and white-striped paper bag brimming with treats, a huge grin on her face.

Other imaginings came and went. Min skipping along a rocky shoreline. Anxious barking at a crab that scuttled across the sand. The three of us running towards an ice-cream van as the jingle played. Strange mishmashes of images where one moment we were swimming, the next sunbathing, Min's bronzed skin glistening with sunscreen only to be replaced with her in a thick jumper and a raincoat but still smiling despite her soaked hair.

But not once was I truly alone, and I wondered if that was how it would always be. I hoped so. Not because I couldn't handle being alone, I was sure I could cope, but because I didn't want to be. I wanted what I once had, and what I had now, which was them. Us. Together.

I cricked my neck as I did that weird thing where you wake from a half sleep and jump like an evil clown has confronted you and said, "Boo!"

"Nice sleep?" asked Min with a warm smile.

"Weird. I wasn't properly asleep, just daydreaming, and I kept seeing strange things."

"Nothing too strange, I hope?" Min sipped her wine; I guess she hadn't dozed like me.

"No, just like photos. Snapshots in time of things that haven't happened. Maybe premonitions?"

"Max, you're acting strangely."

"I didn't mean to. I was just in that peculiar dream state. It was images of us three doing things. Walking, laughing, you buying sweets, Anxious' ears flapping in a gale. Fun stuff."

"That's alright then," Min said as if from far away.

When I turned to reply, her eyes were shut and her drink was close to spilling, so I took it from her and put it on the table.

As she snored quietly, I watched the wind blow the trees and wondered if I could ever be happier than I was right now.

Chapter 15

"That was incredible," gasped Moose, sitting on the blanket with his empty plate nestled in his lap.

"Are you sure you've had enough?" asked Min.

"I'm sure." Moose patted his ample belly and laughed as he said, "There's always room for more, but I'm full, and although I'm a large man I don't eat too much in a single sitting."

"It was a stunning dish," said Dubman as he patted his own stomach and leaned back in the camping chair, sighing happily. "How do you do it, Max? How can you possibly make chicken that tasty?"

"And all done in a single cast-iron pot. Incredible!" added Moose.

"Thanks, but it was no big deal. Just a basic Italian hunter's dish. Peasant food, like all the best dishes. Simple ingredients that truly shine when you treat them with respect. I'm glad everyone enjoyed it."

"But what's the secret?" asked Dubman, leaning forward but groaning as his stomach was so full. "How do you elevate things to the next level? I'm a decent cook, but it never tastes like that."

"You just have to taste regularly and make adjustments. Most people will add the ingredients when they're supposed to, then that's it. But I always use caution and follow the most important lesson I was ever taught when it comes to cooking. You can always add more, but you can never take anything out. So I wait, and let flavours develop, then add a little more of this, a splash of that, until it's just right. Easy."

"He's being bashful," laughed Min with a smile for me, pride in her eyes which filled me with joy and quite a dollop of smugness. "Max was at the top of his game as a chef for years and never lost his touch. He's gifted. It's why the best restaurants were always fighting over him. Did you know he actually had a man following him because a restaurant wanted to offer him a million a year to cook for them, and a big house with a swimming pool and lots of other stuff?"

"And you turned it down?" asked Dubman. "Respect, dude. That's seriously sticking to your guns."

"I left that world behind and will never go back," I said, looking at Min as I spoke, although she'd heard it enough times already.

"Good for you," said Dubman, a renewed sense of admiration in his eyes. "Stick it to the man. Go your own way. Don't get caught up in the promise that riches equal happiness. They don't."

"You sound like you're speaking from experience," said Moose, having fallen into conversation with Dubman easily when they met earlier, seeming like old friends within minutes.

"I sure am," said Dubman, open and breezy as always.

"Care to share?" asked Min.

"Of course. You know I'm from St Davids, and it isn't exactly a place with much opportunity outside of the tourist industry?"

"That's the main source of income for most residents, isn't it?" asked Min.

"It is. Well, I figured out a way to make a fortune away from that industry. I built up this massive online business, but it began to stress me out no end and one day I realised that I was wasting my life. I had money, but I had no time to enjoy the simple things. It was just work and more work and never a moment to myself. I stared at a screen all day long and even when I'd finished work I'd still be glued to one device or another. Stressing over socials, scrolling endlessly, obsessively checking emails and phone messages, and I quit the lot. I sold the business, sold my house, bought the campervan, and lived in it while I renovated it."

"Was it in bad condition when you bought the VW?" asked Moose as we studied the beautiful matt black eighties campervan.

"The worst," he guffawed, a deep belly laugh that showed how genuine a man he was. "It had been gutted basically, and I had to learn welding, spray painting, and source all the interior fixtures and fittings to restore it to how it should have been. Mind you, it's totally unique. You won't find another like it."

"And was it worth the effort?" asked Min. "If you had money, why not pay someone to do it?"

"Because I wanted to prove to myself that I could do it. That I could survive with just the basics, and do something just for me. Does that make sense?"

"Totally." I reached over and slapped palms with Dubman. We both got that we were kindred spirits with an astonishingly similar approach to life, and maybe a past that was similar too.

"Thanks. So, now I roam, and I know I'm luckier than most because I don't have to work as I made some investments with the money I had, but for many vanlifers things are very different. I've met a lot of folk over the last year, and it goes from those like you and me, Max, who want to escape the stress of regular work, to people who simply can't cope with everything that comes with running a house. All the bills and responsibility gets too much for some."

"It's a lot to handle," agreed Min.

"Exactly. And now there's a different way. But the majority of the travellers I meet are those who want to break free from regular life and have more money in their pockets at the end of the month. They still work, mostly online, and plenty work hard, but they don't have to spend it all on their home. Plus, you get to enjoy the beauty of the country. You see so much, and the trade-off is more than worth the sacrifice it takes to live this life."

"You're preaching to the converted," I said, knowing exactly what he meant and having had a similar experience with the mix of people I'd met.

"What about you, Moose? Where do you actually live?" asked Min.

All eyes focused on our mysterious friend, and I realised we knew absolutely nothing about him beyond that he worked security and travelled a lot for work, but where he lived whilst on the road, and when not working, was a total mystery.

Anxious emerged from under Vee and leapt into Moose's lap then settled as the big guy stroked his back gently, his large hand almost covering Anxious' body.

"I'm always on the road, so don't have a home."

"What about parents?"

"Yes, I had parents." Moose smiled wistfully, his eyes closing for a moment, making him look serene, but there was a sadness there.

"You don't now?" I asked.

"I'm a loner, with no ties, and a past that is constantly changing."

"What does that mean?" asked Min, pushing him for more information. "That's totally cryptic."

"I know," he giggled, his round cheeks reddening as he winked. "I've learned so much, become something different to what I once was, and every day I change more, so my past changes, too, as I am no longer that baby, that child, that teenager, or that man. I am Moose. That is all." Moose cradled his hands and rested them gently on Anxious who grumbled happily.

"You're one mysterious dude, Moose," laughed Dubman, slapping him on the back then staring in astonishment at his hand. "Whoa! That was like hitting a brick wall."

"I'm large, and overweight, but there's plenty of muscle too." Moose flexed a bicep, the muscle popping, and grinned.

"So how do you live?" asked Min, seemingly determined to get an answer. "Where do you sleep? Do you have a campervan? A motorhome? A car even? How do you get around? How does it work with your company? Do they drive everyone to the events or do you make your own way? What about in the winter?"

"People always need protection. I go where I need to be, whenever I need to be there. I sleep when I'm tired and can do that anywhere. I study my craft, and practice what I learn."

"I give up!" declared Min, laughing as she threw her arms in the air.

"I like you, Moose," said Dubman.

"And I like you. But now we need to turn our attention to recent events. We need to discover who killed Leanne and Gaz. I'm meant to protect people from bad things happening and I didn't."

"It's not your fault," I said. "Nobody could have saved them, as nobody knew they'd be killed. Even with your, er, special skills, you couldn't have possibly known this would happen."

"No, but now I do, and I want to solve this awful crime. Who does everyone suspect?"

"Don't look at me," said Dubman. "I haven't even met most of the characters you guys have been talking about. I'm just going by what you've already told me this evening. Personally, I would say the most likely candidate is Lash. He had a thing for Leanne, and she clearly didn't feel the same way, so maybe he tried one last time and got angry with the rejection, so decided to kill her."

"That's an extreme reaction," noted Min.

"Sure it is, but killing is always extreme. Or maybe he wanted to cash in as his business is suffering and figured this would draw the crowd. It certainly did, right?"

"But why kill Gaz?" I asked. "He must have known that two killings would ensure the fair was shut down. I can't imagine he'll be allowed to re-open now. The teams will be all over the fair tonight looking for clues and trying to figure this out, so no way has it helped his business. Just the opposite."

"Then maybe it's the competition." Dubman shrugged. "Maybe a rival did it to get him out of business. Mate, it's what I'd do." We stared at him, aghast. "I mean, if I was going to commit murder. Not that I ever would."

"Or maybe it was you," said Moose, his voice so quiet I almost missed it.

"You what, mate?" Dubman whirled on Moose and demanded, "You take that back."

Moose remained calm and said, "You turned up just when this all happened, and how do we know it wasn't you? Maybe there's something in your past that explains why you did it."

"Maybe there's something in your past. You're the man of mystery, not me."

Slowly, a smile spread across Moose's face, and both men began to laugh.

"You were teasing?" asked Min with relief.

"Of course," said Moose. "Dubman's a good guy. I can tell. I'm an excellent judge of character, and don't think for a minute Dubman did it."

"You had me going there, buddy." Dubman shook his head and smiled at Moose, but it had clearly rankled. I wondered how he would have reacted if Moose hadn't been joking but had pushed things further.

"Sorry about that. Sometimes I joke around, but I know now isn't the time. That was in bad taste, and I apologise."

"Mate, no need to apologise. We hardly know each other and you were testing me, I get it. But let's get real here. It could be any number of people, and what we need is to discover the motive. Or find some clues. We need clues. Do we have any?"

"None," I admitted. Although something was beginning to form; I could feel it. A familiar nagging at the back of my mind that I had already met the killer and seen or heard something that would explain everything. "At least," I said cautiously, choosing my words carefully, "nothing that we believe is a clue. That doesn't mean we haven't seen something though. It's just that we didn't know it held any meaning."

"Now who's being cryptic?" chuckled Moose.

"Yes, sorry. The motive could have been any number of things, but that means there has to be a connection between Leanne and Gaz. As far as we're aware, there isn't one beyond them knowing each other a little because he helped set up the small cannabis farm Leanne had."

"That has to be the connection, and the most likely reason they were killed. A rival drug gang," said Dubman.

"But she was small scale and gave it away to neighbours," I said. "You're right that it seems like the most obvious reason, and they must have known each other fairly well for him to have helped her with the growing setup, but it doesn't feel quite right. We're missing something."

"Like what?" asked Min, watching me closely as though she expected something to happen.

"Something that connects them beyond this strange decision to grow illegal drugs in a field of wheat and give it away to the neighbours. I still can't believe Leanne's mum grew it. Why take the risk?"

"Because she liked to get high?" suggested Dubman with a wink and a laugh. "But seriously, she was just one of those people into herbal medicine and realised it helped. It's no big deal."

"It is if you get caught," Moose reminded him. "But let's say the drugs aren't the connection. It still means they knew each other quite well. Well enough for her to trust him to keep quiet about things. Maybe he didn't. Or maybe there's another reason they were both killed that has nothing to do with any of that."

"Which means we've got absolutely nowhere," said Min, her disappointment clear.

"We're getting somewhere," I assured her. "Things are slowly falling into place."

"How can you say that?" she asked. "We haven't come up with anything."

"Not yet, but we will. I can sense it."

"Me too," said Moose. "You get a feeling and all of a sudden everything makes sense. Something you took no real notice of before suddenly pops into your head and everything becomes clear. That's how it works."

"Exactly!" I agreed.

"I get it with my training," said Moose. "I learn something, and yet can't seem to perfect a move, then suddenly it all falls into place when a tiny piece of information I thought irrelevant suddenly takes priority and I have become a master rather than a student."

"For example?" asked Dubman.

"Being somewhere different than expected."

Dubman jumped from his chair and spun to Moose who was sitting on the ground behind him, rather than on the blanket where he was a moment ago. Anxious was still asleep in his lap.

"That… that's not possible. How… you were… Hey, that is so cool!"

"Thank you," said Moose, but after glancing away for a mere moment he was now standing next to Vee with Anxious draped over his shoulder, and still asleep!

"Man, you are freaking me right out," said Dubman, wiping at his forehead.

"All I'm trying to say is that sometimes it takes a while for you to understand something that deep down you already knew." Moose joined us and settled on the blanket again. Anxious slid from his shoulder into his lap like a snake, but remained fast asleep. I was more shocked by that than anything else.

"Moose, you are a true enigma," I laughed, astounded by him yet again. "I understand you want to keep your past private, and how you live your life now, so just know that we are your friends."

"Thank you, Max. That means a lot. See you soon."

And with that he was gone. Anxious continued to snore from his position on the chair, but there was no sign of Moose.

"Is he coming back?" asked Dubman.

"I don't think so. Not today, anyway. I still can't believe he's a real ninja."

"He is? Like, for real?"

We explained about meeting him before and what'd happened, and that nobody recalled him then and even now people seemed to forget they'd met him. When we'd finished, Dubman was silent for a while, then he frowned, shook his head, and asked, "Um, what were we just talking about?"

"You can't remember?" asked Min, glancing at me.

"Nope," he said happily, as if waking from a dream. "Anyway, thanks so much for dinner. It was awesome. It's been so relaxing just the three of us and Anxious. He's adorable, and so well-behaved. Nights like this make vanlife so worthwhile. Hanging with new friends, eating great food. A truly memorable night."

I said nothing, but once again Moose had managed to erase himself from someone's memory. I wondered how many people in the country actually recalled him at all, and if that meant he was lonely. Somehow, I got the feeling that he wasn't, and understood that he would always be his own man and would live life by his own mysterious rules, whatever they might be.

Dubman thanked us for dinner and the enjoyable evening once more, then left, leaving Min and I to discuss the evening and our newest friend. There was more to Dubman than he was letting on, and something about him appearing at the same location as me was nagging at me. Not in a worrying way, but I couldn't help wondering if he had an ulterior motive for being here, or was I merely paranoid because of my stalker and the most recent deaths?

Chapter 16

Once the outdoor kitchen was spick and span and just how I liked it, much to Min's continuing amusement, we settled in the chairs with a frosty glass of Prosecco and sighed simultaneously.

"That was a lovely evening," I said. "Thank you."

"You're more than welcome, although you did the cooking and most of the cleaning up afterwards."

"I enjoy it. You know that. But the company was great and I love having you here with us. Makes it feel complete."

Min sipped her wine to hide her smile, but I knew she'd had a special evening too.

As we sat in silence, a creak made me turn, then something pinged and half the sun shelter, although I was regretting not calling it a gazebo now as it was becoming more a rain shelter than anything, collapsed, one side caving in, only held in place by the pegs and the guy ropes.

We jumped to our feet as Anxious barked at the gazebo—I made up my mind on the name—his hackles raised.

"What happened?" gasped Min. "Are we under attack?"

"I don't think so." I checked the collapsed side and

noted that one of the poles that slotted together had snapped, revealing the cord that ran through the entire section. "The pole just broke."

"That shouldn't happen. It's new. Maybe someone tampered with it? It's sabotage!" Min glanced around, eyes wide, but I laughed. "It's not funny, Max."

"It happens," I shrugged. "Sometimes the poles can snap. They're under a lot of tension and over time can become brittle. It shouldn't have happened already, but the heatwave most likely affected them."

"What are we going to do? It's no good like that, and without it we can't have the outdoor kitchen and will be stuck in the campervan."

"Don't worry, I've picked up a few tips over the last few months, so have a plan. I bought a repair kit with spare poles. We'll have to dismantle the one section, but it shouldn't take long."

"How can you repair the broken pole? They're attached to each other."

"It's meant to be easy. You undo the knot in the end of the cord and thread it onto a new one. Simple."

We dismantled the long section, which caused the rest of the gazebo to topple sideways, but it would be a simple matter to erect it again once the repairs were made. I grabbed the spare poles and the repair kit, rather dismayed to discover all it consisted of was a new cord for if I needed it, and a very flimsy piece of wire with a hook on the end. I read the instructions, which were beyond basic, then explained to Min what we had to do.

It was not as easy as it seemed. We had to take apart the poles then stretch out the cord between the broken one and the next pole, then Min kept hold of it while I pried the end off the first pole. The wire was inserted and it took forever to hook the cord, but I managed it eventually then pulled it free and undid the knot.

"Don't let go of the cord," I warned. "If you do, it will ping back through most of the poles and we'll have to try to thread it through them all."

"Don't worry, I've got it. But how do you thread the cord through?"

With a frown, I read through the instructions, and was dismayed to find that I needed to use another piece of wire and secure it to the cord somehow, then push it through the pole before tying the knot on the end of the last one and replacing the metal cap.

I hunted around in my tool kit, found a roll of suitable wire and some electrical tape, then removed the broken pole.

"Ow!"

"What did you do?"

"I got a splinter from the fibreglass. Wow, it's unbelievably sharp. These things should come with a warning." I managed to pull out a nasty sliver from my finger, then sucked on the blood before wrapping a tissue around the wound that refused to stop bleeding.

It made securing the wire to the cord awkward, but I did it eventually, then used a new pole and began threading.

"Will it work?" asked Min, still holding on to the cord so I had enough slack to play with.

"Should do. It's a tight fit, so lets keep our fingers crossed."

Anxious took this moment to play, and assumed that because Min was on the ground she definitely wanted to play, too, so he jumped at her, grinning mischievously. She lost her hold and the cord snapped back along the poles as we groaned and Anxious wagged.

An hour later, I'd managed to thread the cord back through each section and finally tied the knot with a grunt of satisfaction. I tapped the metal cap back into place and grinned at Min as I said, "You can let go now."

"Are you sure? I don't want to have to go through that again. What a nightmare."

"The joys of camping and using modern lightweight equipment. In the old days it was heavy metal poles, but at least they wouldn't snap."

"Let's get everything back in place so we can chill out. That took ages."

Within several minutes we were sitting in our chairs and clinked glasses, then sipped with considerable smugness.

"What are you smiling at?" I asked Min who seemed way too happy after what we'd just gone through.

"We had a problem and we solved it. Together. Skills like that are important, and we'd never done it before but still managed to fix it. I'm proud of us."

"It was only a broken pole."

"That's not the point. Most people wouldn't be able to do it and would have bought a whole new set already threaded. But we made do with what we had and didn't waste materials. That's a good thing."

"It is," I agreed. "And you're right. It's important that we can do these things for ourselves. I've learned so much about this life, and having the knowledge and skills to make repairs is important. And now we have our gazebo for the rest of the evening."

"Gazebo?" Min raised an eyebrow.

"I know I called it a sun shelter, but that seems dumb now. These things have so many different names, but gazebo it is."

"I like it! But it better not break again." Min grabbed a guy rope and gave it a good wobble, grinning at me the whole time, then with a satisfied nod she resumed her seat and picked up her drink.

"Cheers," I said as I took mine and we clinked glasses again.

"Cheers."

Anxious hopped onto my lap, and our little family admired the gazebo. After we finished our drinks, and with it properly dark now, we headed to the facilities to prepare for bed. Joy had somehow managed to find the time and the inclination to give everything another clean, so the place smelled nice and was gleaming under the strong lights.

When we'd finished, we returned to the van with Anxious trotting along happily, but as we got closer he began to growl and his hackles rose before he tore off ahead, barking.

"Anxious, quiet!" I whispered, concerned he'd disturb the few other guests. He raced back to us and I asked, "What's wrong? But no barking. Show me." With a confused look at Min, we followed him around to the front of Vee to find an envelope pinned behind a wiper.

"Another note," I sighed, looking around but knowing it was no use and my stalker was already long gone.

"Anxious, find the man," said Min, grabbing my arm tight and huddling close.

Anxious sniffed the ground by Vee, then veered off towards the woods. We waited in silence, not a sound from the sleepy campsite, but he returned a minute later with his tail down and his ears pinned to his head.

"It's alright, buddy. You can't win them all," I consoled, wondering how my stalker managed to always elude Anxious who was usually excellent at tracking.

Anxious whined and lowered his head, then sat and waited while I took the envelope and unwound the familiar string. "I can't see inside. Let's move into the light."

We shifted over to the gazebo and the light hanging from the hook in the middle and peered inside. "What is it?" asked Min.

"I still can't see. I'll empty it out." We squatted and I opened the envelope onto the small fold-out coffee table. "Pins?"

"Why would anyone leave pins?"

"Why leave teeth and glass and razor blades either?" I wondered, wishing this nightmare was over and we could be left alone. My heart hammered, I was sweating, and felt utterly exposed here and concerned for Min and Anxious. This had gone on too long and I was at my wits' end. This person was ruining my life. I finally had to admit that. They were scaring me and I knew that Min was unnerved, so I simply had to put an end to this.

"Max, I don't like this. It's frightening."

"I know, and I'm sorry. I don't know why, but this person really has it in for me. It's not normal behaviour and they've got a serious issue. I'll sort it. I promise."

"But how? You don't know who's doing it."

"No, but I'm going to find out. One way or another, this is going to end, and tomorrow. I'll sort it."

"I trust you." Min gathered up the pins and returned them to the envelope, then I fastened it and stored it with the other threats in my now overflowing drawer. Outside, Min was clearing away the wine and glasses so I kept close until she was done, then we got inside Vee and I made sure to lock us in.

Snuggled in bed, I found it impossible to enjoy the closeness, and I knew Min felt the same. She was restless, and kept disturbing Anxious as she cuddled into him but kept moving about. Eventually, she settled and fell into a deep sleep.

I remained awake, going over and over the various envelopes, their contents, and the notes I'd received, trying to piece the clues together and find a common thread. I couldn't figure any of it out beyond the fact the person doing this was a skilled tracker, good at covering their tracks, and had a real thing for fancy brown envelopes. And the aftershave. The unmistakable scent of the same aftershave each and every time.

As dawn beckoned, I fell into an uneasy slumber, thinking about my stalker and the recent deaths, everything getting jumbled and confused as my brain became overloaded with snippets of conversation, clues, and panic at the possibility of harm coming to Min or Anxious.

When I woke, one name popped into my head instantly and relief washed over me as I sat up to find I was alone. Birds were singing and a gentle breeze wafted through the open door, and for a moment I thought something bad might have happened, then heard Min humming before the kettle whistled and she hurriedly turned it off. I settled back and considered the name I'd just summoned, and smiled as several pieces fitted together. I had my stalker, so at least one mystery was solved. Why he'd done this I had no idea, but today I would find out, and put an end to this madness.

With little time to think things through properly, I grabbed my phone and called Dubman to explain as best I could. He said it would be a breeze to track down the person, and he promised to dig up whatever he could on him then get back to me later on. Hanging up, I felt beyond relieved that this would soon be over, and slipped on my shorts then exited Vee with a spring in my step.

"What's got you looking so chirpy?" asked Min as she looked me up and down and shook her head.

"I'll tell you over coffee, but why are you looking at me like that?"

"Max, summer is over. It's autumn now, but you refuse to accept it."

"And I won't until my knees turn blue from the cold. Until then, I'm going to wear shorts and Crocs as long as I can. It's warm today, though, so what's the problem?"

Min flushed as she glanced at me again, and I grinned. "You stop that!" she warned.

"You want me to put my vest on? Don't want to get too hot and bothered looking at my body?" I teased.

"As if! It's just not appropriate for morning coffee," she giggled, before turning away to pour the water.

"Whatever you say." I winked at Anxious who came over for his morning fuss.

Settled with our drinks out in the morning sunshine, it was easy to believe it was still proper summer, but the truth was there was a chill in the air even though it was a glorious day, and I knew it could change to overcast or wet at any moment. Still, I resolved to do as I'd said, and wear as little as possible until the time finally came when shorts and vests would be packed away for good until next year, which felt like such a long way away now.

Would it really not be until next year when Min would be here every morning when I woke up? What could happen in the meantime? So much had already happened, and I'd only been living this life for a single summer. What would I have been involved in by next summer, having gone through the autumn and winter, then the joys of spring, before the best season of the year crawled around again?

"What should we do today?" asked Min as she handed me my coffee.

"Thanks. I'm not sure. What were you thinking?"

"That we should return to the funfair and see what's happening. Think it will be open today?"

"I can't imagine so. But who knows? The two Susans act in mysterious ways, so nothing would surprise me. Can we check on Joy and Rupert too? See if they've come up with anything. And I'd like to meet up with Moose. He's sure to be at the funfair even if it's closed. The contract for security isn't up until tomorrow, so I imagine they'll be asked to patrol the site today and keep things in order and help if there's trouble."

"Think there will be?"

"If the fair's closed, there are sure to be a few angry groups later on or this evening. People will want to come and see where the killings happened if it's anything like yesterday, and I bet Lash will be spitting about losing out on so much revenue. Maybe someone will have news and we can finally figure this thing out. I can't seem to join the dots with any of it."

"That's because you can't focus as well as usual because of your stalker."

"Maybe. Or maybe it's because this time people were killed and the reason is so outlandish that nobody will ever figure it out."

"I have faith in you, Max. You'll get there. You always do."

"Let's hope so for everyone's sake. I hate that Joy had her aunt taken from her, and I can't believe that such a young man was killed so brutally. Why would anyone do that to them? It's beyond comprehension. We need to figure this out before someone else is killed. All the funfair workers must be stressed beyond belief. You wouldn't want to work there at the moment."

"Or visit, but that didn't stop people, did it? I mean, why go somewhere there's a killer on the loose?"

"Don't forget, that's exactly what we did. Our intentions might have been different, but think how much danger we were in. We were right where it happened to Gaz, and that's not good."

"Which is why we need to go back there and see what we come up with. It's weird, but I've got this feeling that we've already seen or heard something that tells us who did it, but I can't seem to hold on to the thought and figure it out. That's how you feel until you solve it, isn't it?"

"Usually. There's this nagging at the back of your mind and it's like you're reaching out but it's just out of grasp. Leave it to simmer, and soon it will boil over and you'll have your answer." I smiled at Min, proud that she was so brave when there was obviously a dangerous maniac on the loose and we were right in the firing line because we refused to give up on our friends even if it meant putting ourselves in danger.

We had a second cup of coffee and a light breakfast before getting ready for the day, then milled about at our pitch, putting off the inevitable, before heading off into town for a mooch around the shops. We'd get a light lunch after that, then visit the funfair to see what was happening.

I don't think anything could have prepared us for

what we found when we finally arrived. It wasn't until two that afternoon, after having discovered a delightful cafe and sitting outside to eat our lunch by the river where swans drifted on the slow water and the sun shone brightly.

Chapter 17

"What happened?" gasped Min as we approached the town hall surrounded by the funfair.

"Bloody vandals, that's what," sighed Lash, tugging at a white vest covered in oil stains and what looked like egg yolk. I guess someone had a fry-up earlier.

"They did all this?" asked Min, taking in the devastation.

"No. I did it after my brekkie!" snapped Lash, tugging manically at his earlobe then clenching his fists.

"Sorry. That was a dumb question. When did this happen?"

"About an hour ago. A group of men came and went wild. They had baseball bats and steel poles and began tearing into everything. I'm ruined. Utterly ruined."

"It's not that bad, surely?" I asked, staring at the mess of cables ripped from the kiosk that ran the haunted house and several other rides.

"It's an absolute nightmare. These machines are old and need careful handling. Look what they did to the wiring. It's impossible to fix."

"Now don't be so pessimistic," said Sheena, shaking her head as she stared at the ruined kiosk. "We'll get one of the guys to fix it no problem. You know Frank is a whizz with electrics. He'll figure it out, and we'll be up and running again in no time."

"Not here we won't," grumbled Lash.

"Did they close you down yesterday?" I said.

"Course they did! What is with you two and the idiotic questions? You still think you can solve this, eh? Well, how about starting with who trashed my business? Those guys ran riot."

"Who were they?"

"Mate, I got no idea. Just a group of nutters who wanted to utterly destroy stuff. We were lucky one of the coppers called it in and they ran off. Otherwise, they would have torn through the whole place. They already ruined the haunted house. Went in there with their weapons and smashed it to pieces while half of them got into the kiosks for the rides and ripped out the wires or just smashed stuff with pipes. We couldn't do anything. I feel like a right loser for not stopping them."

"Lash, don't you talk like that. You did all you could and handled yourself really well. You fought off three of them, but there were too many." Sheena draped an arm around his shoulder and smiled at him, and Lash finally calmed a little.

"You're right. I did what I could. But I don't ever lose a fight and this rankles. Bloody idiots said we were scum and deserved to get beaten to a pulp, but luckily they left everyone alone."

"Yeah, apart from me," moaned Chuck, tentatively prodding his cheek. "I got a right wallop when I tried to stop them trashing everything."

"You were very brave," said Lash with a nod, pride in his eyes. "You stood up for yourself and for all of us. But it was a risky thing to do. I'm proud of you though."

Chuck grew a foot as he stood ramrod straight and beamed at Lash, the swollen cheek and bruised eye proof that he'd tried his best to defend the fair from the attackers. "Didn't want to let them get away with it," mumbled Chuck, bashfully kicking at the ground with a worn boot.

"Good lad. I can't believe this. First the murders, now the place is destroyed. I need a smoke to calm down." Lash fumbled with a pack of rolling tobacco from his pocket and made a very wonky, fat roll-up then stepped away and lit it with a disposable plastic lighter.

As the wheel spun and hit the flint and the lighter burst into flame, Lash sucked deeply on his cigarette and something clicked in my head. I felt light-headed and euphoric, yet saddened, too, as life would now never be the same for quite a few people.

"What happens now?" I croaked.

"Are you alright?" Min squeezed my shoulder. "You look like you might keel over."

"Um, I'm fine. Just felt strange. It's the shock, I guess."

"Lash, what will happen now?" Min asked, frowning at me in concern.

"Now we have to try to fix this mess. I guess the insurance might pay out as this was vandalism, but that's no good to me right now when we have another event in two days."

"This was meant to be your last day here, wasn't it?" I asked.

"Yeah, and the best earner of the year. But that's all gone up in smoke, hasn't it?"

"Up in smoke," I parroted, my voice sounding far away as though I was outside my body.

"What's with you, mate?" asked Lash, squinting at me.

"Just something you said. I think I need to sit down."

Min guided me over to a ride's platform and I sat on the cool metal gratefully. She leaned in close to me and whispered, "I know that look. You figured it out, didn't you?"

"I don't know why, but I know who," I admitted. "I

feel sick. I can't believe this, and for once I feel nothing bad sad. Sometimes you have faith in people, you know?"

"I know."

"And you believe they are caring and honest. I know I've been involved in some horrid stuff, but most people are good. But this…" I shrugged, slowly accepting the truth, wishing it could be otherwise.

"It's alright. Don't feel too bad, Max. You're always so positive and see the best in others, but with what keeps happening it's understandable that it comes as a shock when you figure it out. Are you sure? You aren't mistaken?"

"There's always a chance I'm wrong, but I don't think so. And you're right. I shouldn't be so down. But Min, it's murder. A terrible double murder and those poor people are never coming back."

"That's true, and it's awful, but do what you have to and don't think about that. Think about the lives you will save by ensuring the killer pays for what they did." Min turned away at a commotion, then said, "It's the Susans. We should tell them what you've figured out. We better hurry, as it looks like Lash is about to go nuts on them."

I glanced over, pleased to have a distraction, not pleased to see Lash right up in young Sue's face, her golden jumpsuit shimmering as she put her hands to Lash's shoulders to placate him. He brushed her away and snapped something I couldn't hear.

"Why is he always so angry?" I sighed, hurrying after Min as she ran over, which was both kind and somewhat foolhardy as they were the police and could surely handle themselves.

"Is everything alright?" I asked to try to diffuse the situation as Lash glared at the two detectives who were smiling as usual and strangely now holding hands.

"No, it isn't!" snapped Lash. "These two idiots think the attack on us was no big deal."

"Now hold on a minute, sir," said Susie calmly, adjusting her cardigan with one hand, the other still holding on to her partner's.

"I will not hold on. You haven't done a thing to catch them."

"In case you've forgotten," said Sue with a friendly smile and a shake of her curls, "we do have two murders to investigate. Isn't that more important? We can't do everything at once."

"You can't do anything at all," was Lash's comeback. "You haven't found the killer, and you haven't even got any clues, have you? Go on, tell me I'm wrong. At least give us a little hope that you're going to catch who killed Leanne and poor Gaz. Kid had his whole life ahead of him and you've let his killer go free."

"We most certainly haven't let the killer go free. We just don't know who it is yet. But you can rest assured we're doing everything in our power to solve this case, and fast."

"Rubbish," said Lash, stepping forward.

Anxious growled and rushed to protect the Susans, planting his feet between the two groups, clearly intending to stop Lash.

"Shift that mutt," he ordered, glaring at me.

"Anxious isn't going anywhere, and you need to calm down. It's no use taking out your frustration on them, Lash," I said. "They're doing their best to solve this."

"Really? Look at them. An old granny and an eighties throwback. What kind of detective wears golden jumpsuits? And that much blue eyeliner hasn't been popular since before she was born."

"Don't you dare insult my partner," insisted Susie as she was dragged back by Sue.

"I think he was insulting you too," laughed Sue. "He called you a granny."

"But I am a granny," she said, smiling.

"I know, honey, but he meant you were too old to do the job. Rather lame, actually, as with age comes knowledge and wisdom and you're so smart."

"Aw, that's very sweet."

"When you two have quite finished!" barked Lash.

Anxious gave a warning growl as Lash's fists clenched tighter. It seemed to snap him out of it and he moved back when Sheena tugged gently at his arm.

"Let's all take a breather," I suggested. "And there's something you should all know."

"What's that?" asked a familiar voice, scaring me half to death and making me jump back and take a fighting stance before my brain caught up with who had appeared.

"Moose, where did you come from?" I gasped. "No, don't answer that, as I don't think I'll ever figure you out."

"And who's this fine hunk of a man?" asked Sue, releasing her hold on Susie and straightening her jumpsuit then running her hands through her hair, frowning when they stopped because of all the hairspray.

"Um, it's Moose," Min reminded her.

"Moose? That's an unusual name," purred Sue, shuffling over to him and staring up into his boyish face.

"Very unusual," agreed Susie.

"You really don't remember him?" asked Min.

"No. Should we?" they asked, then high-fived and giggled.

"Yes. You've already met. Remember we told you about him and that he helped with a case at the music festival?"

"Sounds familiar, but I don't really recall the conversation," said Sue with a frown.

"Are these two trying to wind me up on purpose?" asked Lash. "Moose, have you been working your voodoo on them? What's with that?"

"Nothing to do with me," chuckled Moose. "Or is it?" he added cryptically.

"Yes, it is, mate," sighed Lash, rubbing at his face, clearly losing patience again.

"It's how I roll," said Moose with a shrug. "I need to

keep under the radar, and with this coming to a head, I might have peaked too soon and now they don't remember."

"What's coming to a head?" asked Sheena.

"Do you know something?" asked Chuck, rubbing his hands together. "What is it? What's happened?"

"Not me," said Moose. "But maybe you should ask Max."

All eyes focused on me as I smiled at my sneaky friend. "How did you know I knew something?"

"Call it a hunch. Call it a signal in the ninjasphere."

"The ninjasphere?" I asked, unable to stop a smirk spreading. I really did like Moose a lot.

"Yeah, it's a word I made up for when I get this feeling about something. I just got one so hurried right over."

"On your magical flying carpet?" giggled Sue, high-fiving Susie.

"No, on my ninja legs," he said with a frown of confusion. "I might look like I'm slow, but I can get places instantly when I need to."

"I don't doubt that for a second," I laughed.

"So, Max, care to share?" asked Susie, folding her arms across her chest and smiling at me just like Mum did. She knew what she was doing, and played the part so well, but I realised that just like Sue, there was a lot more to this woman than she let show.

"I'm not sure this is the time or the place." I glanced at the others then back to Susie, and she nodded knowingly.

"I understand. Maybe we should go somewhere quieter and have a chat."

"This is why we wanted you on the team," giggled Sue. "See, I said he'd solve it. The famous Max Effort strikes again."

"We knew he was a real catch, didn't we?" agreed Susie.

"What are you idiots babbling about?" asked Lash. "If you know something, I deserve to hear it. We all do."

"That's right," agreed Sheena. "I was working right when poor Leanne was killed, and I had a real soft spot for Gaz. The poor boy didn't deserve this."

"He was my mate," said Chuck, nodding eagerly. "If Max knows who did it, then I want to know too."

"What if I'm wrong? Suppose I tell you what I think happened but it's not true? I don't want anyone to get hurt." My focus was on Lash when I spoke, his anger rising at the thought of getting his hands on the killer.

"You do have a reputation," Sue told him. "We know all about you."

"Maybe I get into the odd scuffle, but that's only because people look down on us. But that's in the past, and it's why we always have proper security now. Right, Moose?"

"That's right. We handle any issues professionally. I told you I could have dealt with the troublemakers, and I would have, but Chuck got to them first when I was about to settle things peacefully."

"Ha, fat chance!" snorted Lash. "I already scared a load of them off, and Chuck was very brave. I didn't see you charging in to break them up and stop them wrecking the place."

"Sometimes patience is important. I was biding my time until they split up, and then I would have handled things with minimal violence." Moose was utterly calm and composed, and I wondered if anything could disturb his seemingly permanently relaxed state.

"We're getting sidetracked here," said Sheena. "Who is the killer?"

"Before I say anything, I want everyone to understand that this is just my opinion. It doesn't mean it's fact. You have to promise not to go on the rampage, and yes, I'm looking at you, Lash. If you can't agree to no violence, then I'm saying nothing to anyone apart from

Susie and Sue. Are we agreed?"

Everyone said that they promised not to do anything rash and that all they wanted to do was help. Chuck especially was keen to get this solved, and explained that he couldn't shake the image of Leanne and that he felt partly responsible because it had happened whilst he was on duty and only a few feet away. It made me shudder when he spoke as Min and I had been in the haunted house, too, and the killer was right there with us.

"So, who was it?" asked Susie, her smart eyes sparkling with excitement.

"Yes, come on, spill the beans!" urged Sue.

I turned to Min and she nodded that I should tell everyone, so with a deep breath I explained who I believed the killer was and a possible reason for the slayings.

"You can't be serious?" growled Lash, his body language anything but calm.

"I'm not standing here and listening to this nonsense," hissed Sheena, taking a step away.

"Nobody is going anywhere," warned Susie, her demeanour changing as she barred Sheena's way.

"Everyone stays right here until Max finishes," said Sue, taking a defensive stance, clearly ready to get physical if anyone tried to bolt.

"I'm sorry, everyone, but they're right," said Moose, his bulky presence suddenly seeming to loom, as though he'd expanded to fill my vision.

Everyone gasped, including the detectives, and Sheena's shoulders dropped as she muttered, "Fine," but she was clearly upset about what I'd said, and I suppose she had good reason to be.

"It's nothing more than a hunch," I admitted. "It was when Lash lit his roll-up that things clicked into place. It makes sense if you think about it."

"You've lost me," said Lash.

"Me too," agreed Chuck. "What's a lighter got to do

with anything?"

"It wasn't the lighter, it was the flame. It got me to thinking about things and how the killer reacted. When I thought back over everything that has happened it all slotted into place. They're sneaky, and very clever, but they made a few mistakes and that's why I'm convinced I'm right."

"Then please share," asked Sue. "We can't go arresting someone just because you got a feeling. Although, I am loving this. Right, Susie?"

"Awesome! It's so wonderful to see a legend in action. He's as good as everyone said he was, isn't he?"

"He sure is."

They slapped palms, enjoying themselves, seemingly oblivious to the way everyone else was feeling.

I explained everything I could, which, admittedly, wasn't much, then Susie nodded to me before turning to the others and warning them, "Do not try to intervene. If we're going to get them to admit anything, we need to play this very carefully. Lash, we're trusting you to leave this to the professionals."

"But he's not a professional, and neither is Moose or Min. Are they being kept out of this too?" he demanded.

The detectives moved aside and conferred in low voices, then returned. Susie said, "Max, Min, and Moose come with us. The rest of you wait here. Do not follow us."

"I'll wait with the others for a while," said Moose, eliciting a nod from the Susans.

Lash was about to argue, but then he nodded and said, "Fine, but you better be right about this."

"Yes!" The Susans slapped palms yet again, then Susie said, "Let's go catch us a killer!"

Chapter 18

We followed the Susans along the country lane, or at least tried to. Susie might have been calm and demure compared to her partner, but when she got behind the wheel it was a different story entirely.

"She's nuts," gasped Min as the red Ford Mondeo screeched around a bend then accelerated up the hill, ignored the junction, and sailed through without even slowing.

"She's definitely not a cautious driver," I agreed, shifting down into second gear and rocking backwards and forwards in a vain attempt to encourage Vee to speed up. "I've never seen anything like it. She's gonna get them both killed."

"It's as though she thinks there's a rush to get there. Why is she driving like such a maniac? Look, there they are. She almost took out the hedge."

"And the car. No wonder the sides are so scratched. She drives like she's only got one speed. Stupidly fast."

"Put your foot down. We don't want to miss it when they confront the killer. I still can't believe it. It's like there has to be another suspect."

"I know it's a hard pill to swallow. I can't imagine what the reason is. Think I'm right?"

"Max, I do think you're right. But hurry up."

"I'm trying. Vee doesn't like hills. Um, or the flat much, but she's great going downhill."

"Apart from the dodgy brakes." Min smiled to show she was teasing, but she had that wild, excited glint in her eyes and I assumed I looked the same way.

"The brakes are not dodgy! They're just special."

"Special brakes?" Min raised an eyebrow and giggled.

"You know what I mean. They take some getting used to is all. You've got it down to a fine art now, but there's no way we can catch up with the Susans." I pressed as far as I could on the pedal and Vee suddenly lurched then sped up.

Min whooped, Anxious whined, and I slapped the steering wheel for joy as we hurtled after the Ford that disappeared around another bend, scraping the dry stone wall as it raced towards our destination.

"We're going to get there just after them," said Min as Vee put on another burst of speed.

I changed into third with the ancient long gearstick, still feeling strange to drive such an old-fashioned vehicle, but I wouldn't have it any other way now and couldn't imagine driving a conventional car. It would feel like I was in a miniature vehicle.

The sky darkened as heavy clouds tumbled in ahead, dark and brooding, obliterating the weak sunshine. The roiling sky flashed with lightning and a moment later a sharp crack of thunder followed by more lightning lit up the fields and hills and shook the campervan before the heavens opened and a gentle rain began to fall.

"That's not too bad," I grumbled, searching for the wiper blade lever as I simply hadn't had to use it much. I found the right control eventually and switched on my headlights, too, something I'd forgotten to do in our haste to leave, but usually always turned on when driving.

"It's just a little shower. I bet it will pass right over us."

Right on cue, the rain turned from gentle to a waterfall and the deluge flooded the road in an instant. It poured in from all sides, running straight off the still hard ground of the fields and racing down the cambered road.

Vee surged on, kicking up spray as we sped after the Ford, but they were lost to sight as the rain become torrential and the wipers couldn't work fast enough to clear the windscreen. I had no choice but to slow down.

"Blimey, look at that!" Min pointed ahead then leaned forward as what appeared to be a tidal wave arced over the brow of the hill, dirty water surging towards us before cascading down the hill like a tsunami on a mission to obliterate all in its path.

The river hit Vee, and I was grateful for our elevated position as the spray reduced visibility to almost zero.

"This is crazy. The road has vanished. It's like driving through a lake." I slowed further and dropped into second, but kept a decent speed as the last thing I wanted was to slow so much that the engine flooded, leaving us stranded. Vee struggled ahead, forging a route through the filthy brown water, leaving us in a murky world the lights couldn't penetrate.

"I can't see a thing." Min leaned forward and peered out of the window, but it was no use and I had to reduce speed to a crawl for fear of crashing. I wondered how the Susans were faring, but found out soon enough as I almost back-ended the now stationary Ford, the water up past the wheel arches as drainage ditches at the bottom of the fields were overloaded and water gushed through gaps in the walls.

Susie must have got it started again as she pulled over into a passing spot where the water was shallow, but the car juddered then stopped again.

Vee stuttered then stalled, and I yanked on the handbrake and put her in neutral before glancing at Min and shaking my head.

"Try and get her started. We don't want to be

stranded," she said.

I turned the key, and although I didn't hold out much hope, I was astonished when Vee spluttered into life, the engine sounding confident and ready to get going.

The two Susans leapt out of the car and waved frantically as they rushed towards us.

"I'll open the side door," said Min as she unfastened her seat belt and climbed into the back.

No sooner was it open than the two women jumped in and Sue got the door closed before the interior was soaked through.

Anxious barked a greeting and the Susans laughed as the door slammed shut.

"Oh boy, that was wild!" chuckled Susie as she shook like Anxious after a shower.

"Crazy," agreed Sue, shaking like her partner.

"Take a seat," I suggested. "Buckle up, then we'll be off. What happened to the car?"

"Engine died." Susie shrugged like it didn't matter as she sat beside her partner and they fastened their seat belts. "Must have been the water. It's like a river."

"I told you to go faster," said Sue. "You were driving like the old lady you are. Too slow."

Min and I shook our heads in wonder but said nothing about Susie's driving as the detectives laughed and Anxious sat between them merrily, enjoying the soggy fuss.

I got going and we splashed through the river of a road, the rain easing as we reached the brow of the hill then sailed down the other side, the water now little but a trickle.

"Now that's what you call a thunderstorm," giggled Sue from the back seat. "It totally did a number on my hair. It's ruined."

I glanced in the rear view mirror to see her trying to tease it out, but it was a limp mess and nothing but a good wash and a few cans of hairspray was going to return it to its eighties stylish glory and she knew it. With a sigh, she just parted it from her face and stared out the window.

"We'll be there in a minute. Does anyone have a plan?" asked Min, nudging me, then turning to the detectives.

"We'll confront our suspect, lay out the evidence, and sneakily force them to confess," said Susie, sounding like she had it all worked out.

"Great idea," said Sue. "We'll get them to admit it, no problem. We have a way with words, and can put on a good show to get people to confess. We always get one in the end."

"You do?" I asked, not surprised.

"Oh yes. Always," said Susie.

"Then let's get this show on the road!" yelled Min above the roar as the rain increased and once again visibility dropped to almost nothing.

I approached the gate to the campsite cautiously, where our suspect awaited us, hopefully oblivious to what was about to happen.

"Are you okay? You're really hyped," I said.

"Fine. Just excited. Is that awful? Am I a bad person for getting a thrill out of confronting a killer? I feel terrible now."

I glanced across and Min looked anything but sullen. She was smiling, her cheeks were flushed, and her eyes were bright. "You don't look like you feel bad," I teased. "You look like you've just come off the best fairground ride ever."

"It's how we get too," said Susie. "You can't beat the thrill of the chase. Gets the adrenaline pumping like nothing else. When you confront someone and get them to admit what they did, it's the best feeling ever."

"Can't beat it," agreed Sue.

I pulled up at the gate and we decided it was best to leave Vee here to block anyone entering or leaving, so I killed the engine. For a moment, all that could be heard was the pounding of the rain and the engine ticking as it cooled. A ground-shaking boom of thunder and a flash of lightning caused us to laugh nervously, the tension getting to us.

Anxious howled as he hated the loud noise, so the Susans consoled him until he settled, then I asked the all-important question. "Are we ready?"

"As we'll ever be," said Susie. "I can't believe we get to see Max in action. This is going to be such fun."

"It really is," agreed Sue. "But everyone be careful. We have an utterly deranged person to deal with and they aren't afraid to use violence, so don't do anything dumb."

"Wise words," said Susie with a smile for her partner as she wrung out her cardigan onto the floor, which shocked me so much I actually tensed up. She stared at the puddle she'd made and gasped before saying, "I'm so sorry. That was beyond rude. I don't know what's the matter with me. How awful. This is your home and I made a mess."

"Thanks for apologising," I said, pleased when she got up and used a cloth to pat the puddle dry.

"I would never normally behave so badly. It must be the excitement. Shall we go?" Susie squeezed out the cloth in the sink, folded it neatly, then with a nod from Sue both exited. Anxious glanced at me, I nodded, and he jumped out after them.

"Ready?" I asked Min.

"As I'll ever be."

"Be very careful. This might get wild," I said, knowing I was smiling.

"You be careful too." Min kissed me, and then we went to go catch us a cold-blooded killer.

Anxious and the Susans were hunched over as the driving rain soaked me and Min as we raced through the open gate. I paused to shut it and caught Min up as she dashed to the house where the others waited. The garden was awash with water drowning the plants and pummelling the once perfect flowers until most were broken or bent over. Wasting no time, Susie knocked on the door of the lovely building. We waited, but nobody came to answer.

With a shrug, Susie tried the door handle and the door eased open. "Hello?" she called. "It's the police. And, er, some others too. Your friends. Max, Min, and Anxious." Still nobody came.

"We better check this out," said Sue, nodding to Susie.

"We should. Everyone inside, but the rest of you wait for us. No wandering off on your own."

We eased inside, sighing as we escaped the rain, and as the door closed thunder boomed and lightning lit up the garden, revealing how bad it had fared with the storm.

Susie and Sue remained together as they checked the downstairs and we waited, but they returned looking confused; nobody was here. They searched upstairs but the house was deserted, so we regrouped and decided we'd have to go outside.

"I think I know where to look," I said. "We should check out the wheat field."

"What's this about wheat?" asked Susie.

"The special wheat we told you about earlier. You know, the drugs," said Min, confused by their forgetfulness.

"Ah, yes, the wheat. Of course." The Susans grinned at each other as if sharing a private joke, but now wasn't the time to ask what was funny as they seemed to find most things amusing, so we stepped back out into the garden just as the rain stopped.

"Wow, a break in the weather. Let's make the most of it," said Sue, already heading towards the field. She turned and asked, "This way, right?"

"Yes, but be careful. It's awkward to get into," I said.

She waited while we caught up, then Anxious led the way through the hidden entry. We ducked down and ran single file through the dense living tunnel, then emerged into the field of wheat.

"It's just crops," said Susie with a shrug. "I thought you said it was a big drug operation?"

"We said it was just twenty plants or so and that Leanne used to give the marijuana away to the locals, but she got help from Gaz and now they're both dead."

"Yes, we know that. You told us. But if that's the case, where is it?"

I took a deep breath, then explained in my best calm voice which way to go, then simply led the way with everyone following.

The sky grew so dark it was almost like night as huge skyscrapers of menacing black clouds roiled overhead and thunder and lightning erupted simultaneously. Anxious whined from behind me, so I turned to check on him and Sue bumped into me, nearly sending me sprawling onto the muddy ground.

"Look at the footprints," I said. "People have just been here. Otherwise, it would be washed away. We should hurry."

"Agreed," said Sue.

Min picked up Anxious and he snuggled in tight as she smiled and caught my eye. "Hurry," she whispered, nodding to the little guy as his tail swished now he was having a cuddle.

"Come on," I whispered, then took the lead again and we strode quickly, but didn't run for fear of slipping on the hidden path between the wheat.

Thunder boomed, then I heard what sounded like a cry. Despite the flooded ground, I picked up the pace and torrential rain was replaced with an incessant tapping as it hit the camouflage canopy above and we were surrounded by the intense smell of the plants.

But all of that was just background noise as I was focused on one thing, and one thing only.

"Stop," I shouted, then raced forward and launched at Joy as the axe she wielded descended towards Rupert who was on the ground, blood pouring from his shoulder, eyes wide with shock and fear as he tried to scramble away from his daughter.

"It isn't how it looks," pleaded Joy, madness in her eyes.

"Liar!" shouted Rupert, using his good arm to prop himself up, revealing a nasty gash to his thigh, the blood flowing freely. He screamed as he tried to stand, and collapsed back onto the dry ground with a thud and another cry.

"I'll kill you!" roared Joy as she raced for Rupert with the axe already swinging again.

I knew in my heart that I wouldn't make it in time, and his skull would be split in two, but I tried anyway, only faintly aware of Anxious barking until he shot past me in a blur and attacked Joy's arm as the axe glinted when lightning flared.

Things got confusing as out of nowhere a black-clad figure emerged from the plants and yanked Rupert aside like he weighed nothing.

Anxious growled through a mouthful of Joy's arm as she shook him about, but he refused to let go. She grabbed hold of him and I saw red and lunged at her and slapped her arm away, then gripped the hand wielding the axe and prized stubborn fingers open. The axe dropped.

Joy spun madly, shaking Anxious, and then a large hand reached out and lifted her off the ground, leaving her dangling like Anxious.

"You can let her go now," I told him, then cradled his body as his jaws loosened and the brave little superstar landed in my arms. He wagged happily and stared at me with love in his eyes and I couldn't help smiling even under such worrying circumstances.

I lowered Anxious and he sat, head cocked, eyes glued to my pocket. With a chuckle of relief, I handed him three biscuits, which made his eyes bug out as he looked from them to me and I confirmed, "Yes, all for you."

Fight over, he lay on his belly and began to munch

on his treats.

"Let me go," screamed Joy, kicking and punching Moose as he stood with his feet apart, face devoid of emotion, merely watching Joy squirm in his incredibly strong grip.

"Let her down," said Susie.

Moose lowered Joy gently and she darted first one way then another, before stopping in the middle of us, nowhere to go. She was surrounded, and she knew it, and I think she'd just given up now that she'd been discovered trying to murder her father.

One question remained.

Why?

Chapter 19

"Glad you made it," I said, slapping Moose's back.

"I like to help if I can," he said with a shrug, then cracked his knuckles.

"A friend of yours?" asked Susie with a raised eyebrow.

"Er, yes. A friend." I realised there was no point going over old ground and explaining they'd already met.

"Very hunky." Sue batted her eyelids and smiled at Moose, the effect somewhat diminished by the fact her makeup had run and her hair looked like Anxious had sat on her head.

"When you've all quite finished," gasped Rupert, wincing in pain.

"Yes, sorry. How unprofessional. I'll call this in." Susie made a quick call then hung up and turned to Sue and asked, "Care to do the honours?"

"Thanks, that would be great!" With a happy smile, Sue read Joy her rights, who remained silent and motionless, the axe still at her feet.

"Isn't anyone going to ask?" Min looked at me than the others.

Anxious barked that he'd like to know the details, too, and focused on Joy now his biscuits were inhaled.

"Maybe you should?" I suggested.

Min nodded, then, face grim, turned to Joy and asked, "Why did you do it? Why kill Leanne then Gaz? And your own father? You were about to murder him."

"My little girl is clearly insane," shouted Rupert, his face red and covered in sweat. He winced as he tried to move again, but although the bleeding had stopped he was clearly in a bad way.

"I don't have to tell you anything," hissed Joy, head snapping up, glaring at us, defiant.

"But you did murder Leanne and Gaz, didn't you?" I said. "There's no point denying it. The murder weapon is right there, and it will obviously match the wounds you inflicted on Gaz. What possessed you?"

"What possessed me? I'll tell you what. She promised me. She said I'd inherit if she died, but she cheated."

"She didn't cheat, and the place would have been yours one day. You were going to move in with your aunty and things would have been great for you both," said Rupert.

"Except it wouldn't, would it? She told me about the dirty drugs she was growing. It's disgusting. Look at it. And you lied! You lied to your own daughter. You were part of it. You make me sick!"

"It was just to earn a little extra money. There's no harm in it."

"What's this all about?" asked Sue.

"Leanne wanted to expand the operation, didn't she?" I asked softly. "But you didn't agree."

"Of course I didn't. She was risking her future, but mine too. If she got found out, the place would have shut down and she'd go to prison or have a massive fine, and then I'd get nothing. I pleaded with her to stop, but no, she was stubborn right to the end."

"Nobody would have ever known," croaked Rupert.

"She needed the money, and so did I. I was going to help her sell it and already had a buyer lined up. It would have been a few thousand each, which we both needed, but you wouldn't listen, would you? Look what you've done."

"I don't care! Gaz turned up wanting to see how the plants were doing, and he said he was going to take over and I'd better not say a word or there would be trouble. He had to go." Joy shrugged like it was nothing to her.

"So you killed Leanne because you found out what she was doing and she refused to stop?" asked Min.

"Yes!"

"But you said you'd just arrived when we found you in bed. And what about the service station? You said you'd stopped there and would be on CCTV."

"Made it up. I knew by the time the police checked it out it wouldn't matter. There was no proof I'd done anything wrong, and I bet nobody even followed up, did they?" she asked, turning to the Susans.

"Actually, no. We failed in our duty and didn't even check to see if you were on CCTV," Susie admitted.

"Because we trusted you and thought you were a lovely girl," said Sue.

"So did we," I said. "Joy, we believed in you, wanted to help, but you killed your own blood and a young man because you didn't want the plants growing here?"

"It's disgusting. It's illegal. They both deserved it. And so did you!" she hissed, then sprang at Rupert who was still on the ground.

Moose was in one place then another, and simply grabbed her and pulled her away, seemingly without effort. He didn't even blink.

"Enough!" warned Susie.

"He's a dirty drug dealer. You know what happened to Alice a few years back and yet you still got involved in this." Joy waved her hands at the six-foot plants growing all around us, several destroyed by her attack and Rupert crawling away.

"Honey, you know everyone was so sorry about what happened to Alice, but this isn't the same thing. You know that."

"No, I made a promise never to touch drugs, and you forced me to break it. You and Leanne got me involved in this even after my best friend overdosed, and that's unforgivable."

"We've heard enough," said Susie, nodding to Sue.

Sue stepped over to Moose and whispered to him, then he scooped Joy up and raced away before anyone knew what was happening.

"Follow me," said Sue, then hurried after them.

"What about me?" wailed Rupert from the ground.

"After what you did to your daughter, maybe you can wait here and think about things until help arrives."

For the first time ever, Sue was serious, and Susie looked even angrier.

"You're really going to leave him?" I asked, amazed.

"He got his daughter involved in something illegal that could result in a criminal record because he wanted to make extra cash. He's fine, and he'll live, so yes, he can wait there until we have a stretcher to carry him out." Susie followed after Sue, and didn't look back.

Anxious sat waiting for instructions, so Min and I used Rupert's torn shirt to wrap his wounds, and although the blood was copious, he would make a full recovery as they weren't as bad as I'd first thought.

"I only wanted to keep my head above water. I never told Joy, but times are hard and cash is tight. Leanne was the same, and struggling, so when I found out about her little operation, I suggested we grow a few more and I could sell it in the city. We didn't mean any harm, and I know it was wrong, but we were desperate."

"We understand, but maybe you should have thought about your daughter first. She asked Leanne not to, but you both did it anyway? You got her involved. What she did is terrible, but you should have looked out for her." Min stepped back from Rupert, and I called after Anxious then left with her trembling as she took my hand.

Rupert didn't call out, or say another word, and I couldn't imagine how bad he felt, and how disappointed he must have been with not only Joy but himself and his sister too.

Rain beat down on us as we exited the tarpaulin protecting us from the weather, and thunder made the ground tremble as we hurried back towards the house. The others were already inside, so we followed Anxious, who looked like a drowned rat, then stepped into the crowded hallway where Joy was sitting on the stairs while the Susans kept a close eye on her.

"Where's Moose?" I asked Min.

"I thought he was behind you? Let's check."

We went back outside as the rain eased off to a fine drizzle to find Moose waiting at the gate. He saluted, and we saluted back, and then a shock of thunder made the windows rattle and the lightning flashed. He was gone.

"You were very brave," said Min, standing on tiptoe to kiss me.

"Thank you. So were you. Are you alright? It's a big shock, and so terrible for everyone involved, but at least it's over now."

"I'm fine. Just relieved to have found the killer. I still can't quite believe it was Joy. She was so nice, and I really thought she was a genuine person."

"So did I. I wish it could be different, but there's no doubt after her confession."

"But how did you know it was her? How did you figure it out?"

"We'd like to know that, too, wouldn't we, Sue?" said Susie as both women appeared then returned inside to watch over a sullen and quiet Joy guarded by Anxious.

"I'll explain, but don't laugh."

"Why would we laugh?" asked Min.

"Because it's so obvious once you think about it."

With everyone looking confused, I stood by the open door and took a moment to study Joy. She looked beaten down and broken, and her eyes refused to meet mine, but there was a determined set to her jaw. When our eyes did finally meet, hers were defiant. She felt she'd been in the right, even though her actions were cruel and terrible. She was clearly not herself, and I wondered how she would feel when the reality of the situation and what she'd done finally hit home.

"Well?" asked Susie, grinning at me like Sue.

"It was when Lash used his lighter. Innocent enough, although smoking obviously isn't the best for you, but when the flint and wheel sparked and the flame appeared, everything made sense. Joy had a real thing about people smoking. She absolutely despised it and couldn't even stand an open flame. It made her attitude to what Leanne had been growing make no sense. She tried to act casual about it, like it was no big thing, but when I thought back there'd been a definite edge to how she spoke and acted about it, and now we know why. Her friend died and she was there. Isn't that right, Joy?"

"Of course I was there. I was with her and she lit a lighter right after she injected this foul drug. She wanted to smoke, then she gasped and just died. I couldn't do a thing to save her. When I discovered what Leanne was doing, we argued, but she refused to back down, so I came up one last time to try to convince her to stop it, but she refused. She stormed off to the funfair and I followed her then put an end to things. But Gaz came up here and threatened me, said he was taking over. No way! He got what he deserved too."

"All that from a lighter?" asked Susie.

"Very impressive," said Sue.

"My hero." Min gave me another kiss, and I couldn't

have felt more loved, even though the circumstances were terrible.

"Most of it was conjecture, but the way Joy acted simply didn't make sense when I thought about it, but there was one more thing that convinced me it was her."

"What?" everyone asked, more excited than they should have been.

"Boobs."

"Boobs?" chorused my captivated audience.

"Just shut up!" demanded Joy, squirming from the stairs where she sat tapping her foot and slapping the balustrade. A tic pulsed under her left eye, but she wouldn't try to escape, as she knew there was nowhere to go.

"Yes, boobs," I said, forcing myself to remain serious and not feel embarrassed, as why should I?

"Are you sure?" asked Min, shooting me a confused look.

Anxious barked a question, so I hurried to explain the rest. "When we surprised Joy in bed and she sat up, she was naked, right?"

"I hardly think we can forget that," said Min.

"And obviously we were distracted."

"I wasn't. But you were, Max."

"Hey, I'm a man, and there were boobs on show. Of course I was distracted. But when I began to suspect Joy, I went over everything in my head and realised one very important thing. There were no clothes in the room. She'd got undressed, but she hadn't left her clothes there. A dressing gown was draped over the chair, but no clothes. Not a stitch. Just a bag that was zippered shut. Nobody gets undressed like that. My guess is that she burned them because they were covered in blood. Am I right, Joy?"

"Just shut up! I'm not saying anything else."

"She probably did," I continued. "All that she had in the room was a bag and her dressing gown. And where were her shoes, eh? She must have destroyed them too.

Remember how hot it was, and that the wood burner was still smouldering? She incinerated the lot. I imagine if we hunt around or check the fire, there will be a few scraps of cloth from then or from after she attacked Gaz. And that explains the bruise on her arm. He got you a good whack, eh?"

"Not really," shrugged Joy. "Idiot used that fake arm to try to defend himself, and all I got was a bruise. No big deal."

"He's done it again!" declared Susie, beaming at me.

"And we got to witness him solving the case," sang Sue, high-fiving her partner.

We were interrupted by the sound of sirens approaching, so with Anxious tagging along, we went outside now the rain had stopped, to wait for the police to arrive.

Once Joy was taken away and the paramedics had seen to Rupert then loaded him into the ambulance and gone to the hospital, Susie turned to me and said, "Well, that's the end to all the mysteries."

"Almost. I have one more thing I need to do. Another mystery to solve, although I think I already have. Time to confront my stalker and finish this once and for all."

"Ah, yes, your stalker. Anything we can do to help?"

"It's all under control, but thanks for the offer. It's been great meeting you, and thanks for letting us help out."

"Max Effort, it was our absolute pleasure."

Both women embraced me in a tight hug, then cuddled up with Min before petting Anxious. He whined as they left with an officer in a police car, and then was silent as they disappeared.

I called Dubman and got the information I needed and plenty more besides, then explained everything to Min before we formed a plan to finish this latest mystery.

Even though we were exhausted, this had to be done now before anything bad happened, so we dried ourselves off, left the officers to begin their investigation, and cleaned out Vee a little before heading off once more.

The night was far from over, and for some life would never be the same again.

Chapter 20

"Are you sure about this?"

I killed the engine and turned to Min as she placed a hand on my thigh, her face full of sympathy. "I'm sure. It's him. I know it is. I can guess at the why, but I need him to tell me and explain why on earth he thought stalking me and sending these cryptic warnings was a good idea. Min, he scared us. I've been so worried something would happen to you or Anxious, and he just won't leave us alone. I have to confront him."

"Then be careful. Shall I come?" Min stifled a yawn, her features hidden by the shadows, the darkness making this feel more dangerous and covert than I hoped it would turn out to be.

"You stay with Anxious and maybe take a nap. We've been driving for hours and I know you're exhausted."

"You're tired too."

"I am, but really wired. Maybe we should have come in the daytime rather than at night."

"No. This was your idea, and it's the right one. There's more chance of him being at home now. But look at this place. Are you sure it's the right address?"

"Dubman was a whizz at finding him. He moved literally a month ago, and he's in terrible trouble financially, which makes his actions even more deranged. A man with no money travelling around the country pestering and threatening me when he should be trying to sort his life out."

"Be careful." Min smiled weakly and squeezed my thigh, then leaned across and kissed my cheek.

"I will." I smiled back at her, ruffled Anxious' fur where he lay fast asleep in her lap, then with a nod I exited Vee and closed the door as quietly as I could. Obviously, it didn't close properly, so I had to open it again and slam it, making me wince and a dog howl.

A cat hissed as it jumped from a pile of black bin bags piled up against the low wall of someone's front garden, the contents spilling onto the pavement. It smelled as bad as it looked, but I kept my nerve and proceeded slowly and cautiously towards the address Dubman had uncovered.

I didn't know this area well, but I knew its reputation, and it had come as a surprise that my stalker lived here. Dubman dug deep and uncovered a rather sad past involving a broken marriage and issues with child support payments. Alcohol abuse and a final collapse of a business and any income had sealed my stalker's fate, leading him to move from a relatively comfortable address because mortgage payments had fallen behind too far and a repossession took place. Now he rented a cheap ground-floor flat in a neighbourhood the residents had tried and failed to elevate from the sorry state it had fallen into over the years.

Several houses were boarded up, others had front gardens full of weeds and cars rusting away on the hard standing. Curtains twitched as people peered out when noise erupted in the distance, and I knew there was a serious issue with knife crime here. I prayed I didn't encounter anyone with a chip on their shoulder or have issues with strangers. I could handle myself, but only to a degree, and didn't fancy my chances against a gang of angry locals with knives.

I relaxed a little as I heard Vee's engine start, and

watched Min drive off as we'd arranged. No way did I want her hanging around here in our lovely campervan. It was asking for trouble. I patted my pocket to double check I had my phone so I could call her when this was over, relief flooding my system when I felt the familiar hard lump.

I turned right at the end of the row of houses and paused a moment at the entrance of a long tunnel. Flickering wall lights bathed the filthy ground in a waxy yellow glow, highlighting layers of amateurish graffiti. But there was nobody there, so I hurried through, holding my breath against the stink where countless late night revellers had stopped for a pee.

I breathed deeply once I emerged into the relative light cast by streetlights, then hurried down the road before moving onto the curb and checking the numbers on the front doors of the three-storey houses. Most were converted into bedsits or flats, with makeshift curtains pinned to windows interspersed with the occasional smart front garden and frilly curtains where the homeowners did what they could to maintain their properties. But most were owned by landlords, hardly any private ownership here, and everyone was struggling to make ends meet.

I found the correct address and paused at the partially open wrought-iron gate broken free from one of the hinges set into the brick wall. Empty plastic bottles and other detritus littered the street and the compact front garden overgrown with a peculiar evergreen shrub that blocked the view through the window.

My heart beat fast as I opened the gate carefully and the remaining hinge squealed, and for a moment I had second thoughts. Was I even right about this? Was this a good idea? What did I expect to happen?

To find peace. That's what I wanted to happen. To stop being stalked and pestered, threatened and followed. This had to end, and it had to end now. I left the gate open and approached the front door where three doorbells had names scrawled on the tiny spaces beneath. I pressed the correct button. A faint chime could be heard through the door, so I waited, trying to get my breathing and pulse under control.

A door slammed and I took a step back, then waited as a lock clicked open. As the door was flung open, the stench hit and I almost gagged, but remained where I was and nodded at the man standing before me, his shoulders hunched.

"I knew you'd turn up eventually," he said. "You better come inside." Without another word, he turned and shuffled along the hall, his brown slippers scraping across the threadbare carpet in the communal hallway where bikes leaned against the wall, and coats hung from cheap plastic hooks. A pile of mail had fallen off a pine table and simply been left where it fell.

My stalker opened the door to his flat and nodded to me that I should follow, so I entered behind him and the door closed with a thud thanks to the fire safety hinge.

The smell faded, replaced with a sickly sweet aroma no amount of pine air-freshener or the distinctive aftershave could disguise. I followed the familiar man along a narrow hall with several doors revealing a basic and surprisingly clean kitchen and a small bathroom, again, clean and organised, but dated and with mould in the corners through lack of available ventilation.

Barry Simms slumped into a tired brown corduroy couch that matched his own brown cords in a worrying way. His brown shirt hung loose, several buttons undone at the top and bottom, revealing pale, sagging skin although he wasn't a large man but clearly had been eating badly, not exercising, and drinking way too much booze. He ran shaking fingers through oily, limp brown hair as he studied me intently whilst pouring a generous measure of vodka from the almost empty bottle on the table in front of him. As an afterthought, he added a splash of orange juice from a carton and slammed half the drink home in one gulp.

Barry wiped his mouth with his sleeve, eyes still locked on mine.

"I'd offer you a drink, but as you can see, I don't have much left."

"What about the unopened bottle on the dining table?" I asked, nodding to the table where books, papers, photographs, camera equipment, and a laptop fought for space amongst the empty bottles and the single full one.

"That's to get me through the night and tomorrow morning," he hissed, eyes focusing back on me. I remained silent, just took in the tired room, the tired man, and the tired atmosphere. Everything was drab, unimaginative, and like he'd given up on everything. "Are you expecting me to apologise? Because I won't." Barry finished his drink, poured the dregs into his glass, and drank it without even bothering with the mixer.

"I'm not sure what I was expecting. It wasn't this, or you, but once I realised it must have been you stalking me, I wasn't sure what I'd find or what I'd say beyond asking you to stop."

"Ha, so the amateur detective beat the real one. You know, I always prided myself on doing a great job as a private detective. It may not have been fancy work, or very well paying, but I had a reputation as a good investigator. People respected me and came to me for help. I always tried to do right by them."

"That's admirable."

"Don't be so condescending!" Barry slammed an arm onto the sofa. Dust billowed and he coughed, his red eyes streaming as he hacked away like a pack-a-day smoker.

"I didn't mean to be. Look, Barry, what's this about? I can see you've fallen on hard times, but why are you picking on me? All those threats, the weird things in envelopes, not to mention the promise of violence. What possessed you? Why me? What did I ever do to you?"

"What did you do!? Are you insane? You know exactly what you did. You ruined my life. You and your goody-two-shoes attitude and your holier-than-thou smugness. You ruined me."

"I have absolutely no idea what you're talking about."

"Liar!"

"Barry, I genuinely don't. You're the one who was following me before, right from the start of my vanlife. Why are you in my life again now? You promised that was the last I'd see of you. That you were just doing your job and following me until your client decided it was time to make me that offer of a job and a nice house if I worked in their restaurant. That's as far as our relationship went. You were following me back then, but I didn't for one minute think you'd be the one responsible for what's happened. Why?"

"I lost everything because of you. Yes, I was already behind with my mortgage and work had dried up. It's hard to manage a house when you have child maintenance to pay, a car to run, and everything else that goes with it."

"I'm sorry that things got so tough for you, but what does any of this have to do with me?"

"I would have got a fat bonus if you'd accepted, and they promised to pay me well regardless, but they welched and paid me a pittance. I don't have the money to take them to court over it, and it was only a verbal agreement anyway. I got nothing and lost my home. Turned to the drink again, which I swore I'd never do, and now look at me. A drunk PI with no clients, no office, and it's all because of you. You destroyed everything."

"I still don't understand. If they didn't pay you, how is that my fault? I'm sorry you missed out on a big bonus if I accepted their job, but you know I wanted to change my life for the better and do the things I knew were right rather than going back to a world I'd just escaped from. That life ruined my relationship with Min, and almost put an end to everything I loved in this world."

"Listen to you! You're not so special, you know? You sound so high and mighty like you've done this incredible thing, but all I see is a dropout who only thinks of himself. What about me, eh? What about my life? My future? You ruined it!" Barry stumbled over to the table, grabbed the vodka, then returned and poured a huge measure into his glass and splashed the remaining orange juice in. With shaking hands, he took a large mouthful. Again, he wiped his mouth with his sleeve, his eyes darting around the room and his leg bouncing up and down nervously.

"How would I have known what would happen to you? I don't know you at all. You can't seriously blame me for not wanting to get stuck in a world I'd managed to escape from."

"You destroyed everything, so I thought I'd give you a taste of your own medicine," he mumbled through his fingers as he rubbed at his face.

"Will you explain what it meant? Why the envelopes? What did the sand and pebbles mean? The glass? The pins? It makes no sense."

"Ah," he said, grinning slyly, "thought you'd be intrigued. Max Effort the big detective and he couldn't solve it. I bet it drove you nuts, didn't it?" he chortled, his laugh turning into a hacking cough he made no effort to cover up.

"I couldn't figure any of it out," I admitted.

"I got the better of you," he grinned. "The pestle and mortar are obvious. A nod to your life as a chef and the job you turned down."

"What about the pebbles?"

"To remind you that not everything is easy, and that sometimes all you get is a bag of rocks."

"And the glass?" I asked, realising that Barry wasn't just down on his luck but was clearly deranged. What he was saying made no sense, but he didn't seem to understand that.

"So you'd think about your life and how fragile it is. I found it on the beach when I was walking, watching you, and you never noticed. Who's the best detective now, eh? I followed you all the time and you didn't have a clue. I'm no amateur," he said smugly, then finished his drink and almost dropped the glass as he fumbled to place it on the table.

"Barry, I don't think you're well. These things make no sense. That's so cryptic that nobody would ever figure it out. It's meaningless. Was there any significance to the razor blades, or was that just an obvious threat of violence? The same for the pins."

"It's because you need to cut that damn beard of yours! Even you must have figured that one out." He shook his head almost sadly, as though he was disappointed in me.

"I assumed it meant you'd try to hurt me. Or Min and Anxious. You scared them. You scared me. That's not smart or clever or anything but nasty and childish. Skulking about like that and leaving threatening notes or things in envelopes nobody knows the meaning of is juvenile. You need help, Barry. You need to see someone and try to get yourself in a better place mentally and physically."

"Don't you dare look down on me! I don't need a lecture from you. I beat you at your own game. I left all these clues for you and you still couldn't figure it out. I beat you." Barry smiled smugly, but it was tinged with a meanness I'd never seen before. He was clearly verging on madness, and I feared for not only my safety, but his.

"I think it's time I left."

"Not yet! You haven't told me how you figured out it was me. I knew you couldn't solve the clues."

"Barry, they weren't clues. Yes, the notes make sense now. That you knew what I did, that you were watching me. That I understand. But pebbles and glass? That's not normal. What about the teeth? Where on earth did you get teeth from? And what did that mean?" I couldn't help myself, and realised that just like him, I hated not knowing the answer to a mystery.

"Ah, the teeth," he tittered, frowning when he checked his glass and found it empty. "I got them off a client. A dentist. Told him I needed them for a job and he didn't even ask why."

"But why leave them for me to find? What does it mean?"

"That I'm going to punch your teeth out, obviously," he said calmly. "And the pins mean a good stabbing."

For a second, he was absolutely still, then in one astonishingly fast movement he pulled a knife from where it was hidden down the side of the sofa and lunged forward, slashing at my stomach.

I jumped back and banged into the table, causing the empty bottle of vodka to crash over then roll onto the floor, but Barry was wild and madness filled his eyes as he darted left and stabbed out, so close to injuring me that for a moment I couldn't move. But as he swiped again, I recovered my senses and the fight reflex took over. I moved without conscious thought, and vaulted the sofa to get some distance and protection as Barry stumbled forward, unsteady on his feet, eyes now filled with utter hatred.

"You ruined everything!" he screamed, then jumped onto the sofa and slashed at me. I moved away easily and he lost his footing then spun as he stabbed out almost blindly. His momentum carried him around and he fell off the back of the sofa and screamed as he landed.

I dashed over to where he was writhing in pain and staring in horror at the knife protruding from his thigh.

"Don't move, and do not try to take it out," I warned. "I'm serious, Barry. Do not try to pull it out."

"How could I?" he wailed. "Help me. Please, do something." His eyes fluttered, he gasped, then they rolled up and he lost consciousness. Barry was so drunk I was amazed he'd been able to move at all, but at least now he couldn't try to kill me.

I took several deep breaths then called the police. When I hung up, I checked on Barry but he was breathing deeply and the wound wasn't bleeding too much so it seemed like he'd survive. Relieved, I called Min and explained what had happened and that it was safe for her to come as the police would be on the scene soon enough.

I returned to the communal hallway, making sure to prop the door open so I wouldn't be locked out, then waited on the step as sirens rang out in the distance for the second time that day.

The night suddenly felt very chilly.

Chapter 21

The next morning an Uber took Min to the station after a lie-in and a hearty breakfast I insisted on cooking. We were sad to see her go, but understood that she had work commitments and the last thing she wanted to do was let her clients down.

Anxious and I took our time getting everything packed away into Vee, and I even made a few adjustments to how things were arranged, finally admitting that shorts, vest, and Crocs weather was now behind us until next year. I was sorry to see my summer attire go, but was also looking forward to what felt like a new chapter in my vanlife.

The struggle was real, and I would face it bravely, and possibly with a thick jumper and a pair of wellies, but I was determined to remain a vanlifer, and would deal with whatever faced me.

With nothing left to do, we took a wander around the campsite, and I lamented the loss of such a beautiful site, but wondered if maybe Rupert would take over things and continue to run it. Maybe I'd come back next year to see, or maybe some things are best left a mystery.

Up at the house, police were everywhere, the garden, and the fields beyond swarming with officers removing the plants and various equipment Leanne and

Rupert had invested in. I didn't have the stomach to inspect the delightful garden as who would tend it now, so we returned to my beloved campervan and I sat and rested, gathering my thoughts, already pining for Min.

Anxious was exhausted, so curled up at my feet and groaned as his eyes closed, taking advantage of the quiet site to get a little shuteye. I simply watched the trees swaying in the breeze, thankful the storm had passed. Like a final farewell, the sun popped out from behind a wispy cloud, the humidity soaring instantly.

"Ah, why not one more day?" I exclaimed, then jumped up, hurried to Vee, and stripped off my jeans and T-shirt and changed into my cutoffs, a green vest, and my battered, well-worn Crocs.

I smiled as I sat back down in my camping chair, happy and content with my life, especially as the sun was shining.

Whatever happened, whatever mysteries I got involved in, I knew there would always be my family to support me. Anxious whimpered as he chased rabbits in his sleep, and I remained still, doing nothing, in no hurry to leave, as what did it matter? I had time on my side, so I let my best friend sleep for an hour, and when he roused and had a drink of water, I reluctantly packed away my chair.

"Where to next, buddy?"

Anxious barked an answer, and I laughed as he sat, head cocked, waiting for my reply.

"Sure. Why not chase the sun a while longer? Cornwall it is. The weather will be better, and we can see the sights. Maybe there won't be any drama for a while. Or maybe there will."

Anxious yipped.

"Yes, you're probably right," I chuckled, "but let's go anyway."

The End

Except it isn't. Read on for Max's awesome chicken cacciatore recipe and a little about what to expect in the next book, Island of Death! Please join me, and let's make a one-pot wonder.

Recipe

Chicken Cacciatore

A classic Italian hunter's stew is the perfect one-pot wonder for when the weather isn't too scorching. Being in the UK means you can usually take it for granted, but the last few years have been so unpredictable that we've gone from a raging inferno to cool and damp in the space of a few hours. It makes camping problematic as one minute you're sweating in your shorts, the next you're hunting through bags of clothes for jumpers and thick socks!

Ingredients

A mixture of chicken and rabbit pieces would be a little more authentic. And you could add some carrot too.

- A chicken cut into 8 pieces (or 12 bone-in chicken thighs), seasoned with salt and pepper
- Olive oil - 2-3 tablespoons
- Onion - 1 finely sliced
- Garlic - 4 cloves minced
- Celery - 1 stick finely sliced
- Red pepper - 2 roughly chopped
- Mushrooms - 250g / 8oz chopped
- Wine - a glass of something dry (red if possible but use what you have)
- Passata - 400g / 14oz
- Red wine vinegar - 1 tbsp
- Dried bay leaves - 3
- Dried oregano - 1 tsp
- Crushed chilli - 1/2 tsp

- Olives - 20 whole black, ideally kalamata because hey, they're the best (or use your favourite)

Method

This is a simple tasty stew. It doesn't take too long and can be eaten with whatever you have to hand. Good bread, pasta, cous-cous, rice, or mashed potatoes will fill you up, or keep things lighter with a big pile of steamed green vegetables.

- Hopefully you have a large, heavy casserole by now. Heat the oil on a high heat, and add the chicken pieces. You want to brown the outsides, so do this in batches if need-be, turning every so often. It should only take 5 or 10 minutes. As the pieces are done remove them to a plate.
- Once all the chicken pieces are golden, remove all but around 2 tbsp of fat and turn the heat down to medium. Add the onion and cook gently for 5 mins or so, to soften.
- Stir in the garlic and give it another minute or so to release some flavour.
- Now turn the heat back up and stir in the vegetables. Sauté for 5 minutes or so until starting to soften and any watery juices have evaporated.
- Add the wine and give it a good stir, scraping up any golden sticky bits from the bottom of your pot. Let it bubble away for a few minutes to reduce a little.
- Pour in the passata and vinegar, along with the bay leaves, oregano, and chilli flakes. Once it starts to simmer, carefully add the chicken pieces, making sure to submerge them in the sauce. Bring it to a slow simmer, pop on a lid, and leave to cook gently for 45 minutes or so until the meat is falling from the bone. Keep an eye on it, give it a stir now and again,

and add a little water or stock if you think it's drying out.
- Add the olives and simmer for another 10 minutes before serving.
- Done, buon appetito.

Salad and really good bread to mop up all that juicy goodness are perfect for this one-pot chickeny wonder.

From the Author

Maybe things will be chilled in Cornwall. Max seems to think so, but Anxious knows better. With the next book titled Island of Death, I can't see it being a very relaxed trip, but we'll just have to see, won't we? Please dive in, and discover what awaits Max and the gang in book ten.

Be sure to stay updated about new releases and fan sales. You'll hear about them first. No spam, just book updates at www.authortylerrhodes.com.

You can also follow me on Amazon www.amazon.com/stores/author/B0BN6T2VQ5.

Connect with me on Facebook www.facebook.com/authortylerrhodes/

Printed in Great Britain
by Amazon